CHRISTMAS KISSES AT THE FARM ON MUDDYPUDDLE LANE

Heart-warming, uplifting romance

Etti Summers

CHAPTER ONE

Eliza York stood to one side as the cabbie lifted her bags from the boot of the taxi and placed them on the ground next to her feet. The ground in question was a rough, asphalt carpark whose surface glistened from the sleety rain falling from a dark, misty sky. She paid him, adding a generous tip, then looked around, pulling her jacket closer as he drove away.

Abruptly she felt very alone. She was in the middle of nowhere, in a strange country, and there wasn't a soul in sight. However, lights shone from the windows of a house beyond the carpark and more lights illuminated a stable yard, so she shook off the feeling and took a deep breath. She hadn't come all this way to let second thoughts get the better of her.

As per the instructions that had been emailed to her by the owner when she'd booked the holiday cottage, Eliza headed for the house, hitching her carry-on over her shoulder and pulling her wheeled case.

Mist swirled around her, and the silence was unnerving as she hurried towards civilisation and the place she would call home for the next two weeks. But as she picked her way along the path, she was forced to wonder whether two weeks was going to be too long.

From what she had seen of Picklewick as the taxi had sped through it, there didn't appear to be much there to maintain her interest. But then again, it was ten-thirty at night, so a little English village was hardly going to be humming with activity, and she **had** spotted a pub that seemed to still be open, so she had a smidgeon of hope that there would be something to do in the evenings.

In hindsight, maybe she should have hired a car – at least she would have been able to travel around a bit – but she'd had the romantic idea that she would see more of the local area if she used public transport. However, she had swiftly changed her mind when she'd got off the train in Thornbury earlier and was informed that the last bus to Picklewick had left over two hours ago. Her journey had been going so well up to then...

Meh, she thought as she trundled her case across the cobbled stable yard; she was just tired and fed up with travelling – she would undoubtedly feel more upbeat tomorrow.

It was a shame she didn't have anyone to enjoy this trip with, but neither her mother nor her sister had wanted to come, and Eliza no longer had a significant other. It was the latter that had been responsible for her impulsive purchase of a plane ticket to the UK, together with a promise that she had made to herself after Dad died. She had originally harboured the hope that she and Archer would make the trip together, but he had decided to bugger off to Australia instead, to work on a sheep farm of all places. As if there weren't enough of the blighters in New Zealand!

When it came to men, she couldn't half pick 'em. After her disastrous marriage to Larry, she swore she would never look at another man again. Then along came Archer and she'd forgotten all about the promise she had made to herself.

Huh, she wouldn't be making **that** mistake again.

As she approached the farmhouse, she was about to knock when she heard a dog bark and the door flew open.

A woman, whom Eliza estimated to be in her early thirties, smiled warmly at her. 'You must be Eliza. Hi, I'm Petra. Come in. Would you like a cup of tea? Coffee? How was your journey?'

A black spaniel darted out from between the woman's legs, its tail wagging furiously, and Eliza bent to ruffle its ears.

'Sorry, Queenie thinks everyone loves her,' Petra said, clicking her fingers. The dog slunk back to its mistress.

'That's okay, I like dogs. Er, yeah, I'm Eliza. Nothing for me, thanks. I just want to settle in, have a shower and get my head down.' She had been travelling for nearly forty-eight hours, and although she had managed to get some sleep on the plane, she was buggered.

'Of course. I'll take you to your cottage. There's a couple staying in the one next to yours, but they'll be gone tomorrow and I haven't got anyone booked in until after the New Year, so if you start to feel a little isolated, feel free to pop up to the house. There's always someone around.' Petra reached for a key sitting on a chunky hall table and picked up a torch.

Eliza gazed at it doubtfully, and Petra noticed her concern. 'Don't worry, there are torches in the cottage if you need them, and there's a welcome pack, too. I've popped in some extra bits and pieces, seeing as you'll be staying over Christmas.'

'Thanks, that's very kind of you.' Eliza hoped milk and tea bags were included, because she couldn't get going without a cup of tea in the morning and she wasn't sure how far it was to the nearest shop. According to her research, it was less than two kilometres, but she wanted to get her bearings first before she ventured further than the immediate vicinity of the cottage.

Petra led Eliza back the way she had just come, but turned off down a little track before they reached the carpark, saying,

'If you want to move your car in the morning, the cottages have their own parking area and it'll save you trekking up to the stables whenever you want to go out.'

'I haven't got a car, but maybe I should think about hiring one? I took a taxi from the train station.'

The woman wrinkled her nose. 'No worries, you can get to Picklewick easily on foot. But if you did want to explore more of the local area, a car would come in handy. At least we drive on the same side of the road as you,' Petra added with a laugh. 'I bet the weather here is a bit different though.'

'You can say that again!' Eliza's reply was heartfelt. She had swapped a balmy New Zealand summer for a freezing English winter, and she wished she was wearing more layers.

As they rounded a corner, a row of three cottages emerged out of the mist. Petra halted outside the middle one and unlocked the door, indicating for Eliza to go first.

A lamp was shining inside, and Eliza stepped into a cosy lounge and gazed around in delight. It was small (she had been expecting that) but a first glance it seemed to have everything she would need. There was a fireplace with a log burner that was kicking out a lovely amount of heat, and there were even Christmas decorations and a sparkly tree in the corner. It all looked very festive, and Eliza suddenly felt homesick. She would be spending this Christmas without seeing her family, and once again she wondered whether she had made the right decision in coming all this way.

Petra was saying, 'There's a booklet in the kitchen with information on the local area, plus my mobile number – although I must warn you that the mobile signal here is dire. If you need anything, it might be easier if you just pop up to the stables.' She handed Eliza the key. 'I hope you enjoy your stay.'

'I'm sure I will.'

Eliza waited for the woman to leave, then she wearily eased the bag off her shoulder.

Knowing that she would be arriving quite late, she had packed a pair of pyjamas in her carry-on, as well as a few toiletries, which meant she could hit the sack without having to unpack her suitcase.

But before she went upstairs, she had a quick look in the kitchen and was touched to find that the fridge contained milk, butter, cheese, and a bottle of Devil's Creek Sauvignon Blanc. Providing her with a taste of home was incredibly thoughtful, and she looked forward to having a glass. A wicker hamper on the countertop held chocolates, a box of mince pies that appeared to be homemade, tea, coffee, bread, jam, and a few other bits and pieces that she was too tired to examine right now.

Yawning hugely, Eliza fished her night things out of her bag and went upstairs, to fall asleep seconds after her head hit the very comfy pillow.

Jay Fairfax peered out at the drizzly night through his sister's living room window and said, 'I hope it will clear up by tomorrow.'

'Snowflake,' Dulcie teased. 'I assumed you would be used to rain, what with spending all your time in a rainforest.'

'Yeah, a **warm** rainforest.' As Jay returned to the sofa and sat down, he continued, 'I don't mind the cold and I don't mind the wet, but not the two together.'

'How about snow?' Dulcie asked. 'It's forecast for later in the week. We might even have a white Christmas.'

Maisie squealed and clapped her hands, and Jay winced. At twenty-five, she was the youngest of his three sisters, and she acted it, too. Jay had forgotten how childlike she could be. Well, he would, wouldn't he, considering he only came back to the UK once or twice a year, so he hardly ever saw her. Although, that might be about to change. If he didn't get another contract, he would be staying in the UK for a while, and that meant moving back in with his mum and Maisie, in the family home in Birmingham.

Dulcie pulled a face. 'I hope it holds off until Thursday because I'm having goats delivered on Wednesday.'

'It's amazing what you can buy on the internet,' their mother said, and Jay raised his eyebrows.

'Please tell me Mum is joking,' he pleaded.

Dulcie laughed. 'I suppose I **could** have bought them online, but I wanted to see them first. The breeder has confirmed that they're all in kid, so in a few months there'll be lots of baby goats running around.'

'I love goats!' Maisie cried. Her expression became dreamy. 'Can I help with them when they have their babies?'

'Maybe – **if** you've not found another job by then,' Dulcie said, and Maisie pulled a face.

Jay caught the look Dulcie gave her, and he guessed the reason. Maisie was notorious for the number of jobs she'd had since leaving school. He had lost track. Whenever he spoke to his mum on the phone, Maisie had either just walked out of a job because it 'wasn't for her,' or she had been 'let go'. He was totally in favour of people trying different careers until they found one that inspired them, but all Maisie did was flit from job to job, sticking at none.

She was nothing like him or her sisters, or Mum for that matter, and if it wasn't for the fact that she had the Fairfax eyes, he might have thought Maisie was adopted.

'Are you going to breed goats?' he asked Dulcie. She was turning into a proper farmer.

'I'll have to see how I get on first. I'm hoping to make soap and other lotions from their milk. And Otto will also use the milk in the restaurant once we get the pasteurisation shed up and running.'

'I can't wait to have a look around this farm of yours,' he said. It had been dark when he'd arrived, the December day having already turned to dreary evening, so he hadn't had a chance to see it yet.

Jay was delighted that his middle sister was doing so well for herself. Not only had she won the farm in some kind of lottery (how had she managed **that!?**) she was also in love with a man who could cook so incredibly well that he had earned himself a Michelin star.

Otto had made the family a fabulous meal this evening, and was now poring over a laptop and scribbling notes on a pad. The fella was opening his own restaurant in Picklewick shortly, and according to Dulcie, he was working flat-out all day every day to get it ready for early January.

During dinner, Dulcie had made Otto promise to take some time off over Christmas, and Jay had seen the reluctance in the man's eyes when he'd agreed. Otto was clearly driven, and Jay hoped his restaurant would be successful.

If his cooking tonight was any indication, it should do very well indeed.

'And I can't wait to show you around,' Dulcie said, pride evident in her voice.

From what he had seen so far, which was only the inside of the house, Jay was impressed. Dulcie had worked hard to make it look nice, and although the farmhouse wasn't modern, it was rustic and cosy. She had painted the plastered walls white, but had left the exposed stone ones as they were. There were thick rugs on the flagstones downstairs and the floorboards upstairs, fires burned in the dining room and the living room, and the place was festively decorated to within an inch of its life.

Dulcie had a large (very large) Christmas tree in the living room, and a smaller one in the dining room, and he had even found a miniature tree in his bedroom. Then there were the garlands, the bunting, the candles, the... He could go on, but there was just so much. Still, it was very festive and she had gone to a great deal of trouble, which he appreciated. He was looking forward to spending Christmas with his family. Good food, plenty of alcohol, slobbing about in his scruffs, and perhaps a party game or two whilst watching a cheesy film on the telly... for Jay, that's what Christmas was all about.

Plus seeing his old mates, of course.

But this year would be different.

In the past, he had always stayed with their mum, sleeping in the little box room that used to be his bedroom when he was a child. For the first few years after he had begun working abroad, visits home had invariably involved catching up with his old mates. But lately, those boozy blokey sessions had become fewer as, one by one, the lads who he had gone to school and college with, had settled down. He still saw them occasionally whenever he came back to the UK, but he was more likely to be invited to a dinner party with their wives or partners, than go for a fun night out in a bar or a club. And over this past year, it seemed as though everyone else had raced ahead relationship-wise, leaving him in the starting blocks.

He wasn't sure whether he envied them, or whether he had dodged a bullet.

He felt a tad envious seeing his sisters so loved up and happy, and a part of him wanted what they had. But was that just

FOMO, or did he genuinely want to fall in love and settle down?

He supposed he might find out, now that his contract had ended and it looked as though he would be staying in the UK for a while until he landed another. He wasn't sure how long he could take living with his mum and little sister though, so the sooner he found another job, the better.

Dulcie, sounding remarkably like Maisie, brought him out of his reverie when she cried, 'Ooh, this is going to be the best Christmas ever!'

Jay seconded that. He also had a feeling it was going to be a Christmas to remember.

Eliza slept for a full eleven hours, and
when she woke she felt considerably more
refreshed than she had expected. No
doubt jet lag would kick in later, but for
now she was keen to explore.

Eager to see what the weather was doing,
she peeped through the curtains and was
delighted to discover that yesterday's
mist had lifted and the rain had stopped.
The view from the bedroom window
across the valley was stunning. Despite it
being the middle of winter and most of
the trees being bare, the overwhelming
colour was green, and it was easy to
imagine how lush the place would be in
summer. Her dad hadn't been
exaggerating when he'd told her how
verdant and vibrant his homeland was.

A pang shot through her as Eliza thought
of her father, and she wondered how

much longer it would be before she could think of him without feeling as though she was being stabbed in the heart. He had died two years ago, but it felt like it was only yesterday when she'd had that awful phone call.

She wished she had been able to persuade her mum to come with her to the UK (it might have helped Mum with her crushing grief if she could see where Dad had lived before he'd emigrated) but she claimed she couldn't face such a long journey. Neither had she been too enamoured of Eliza's desire to fly halfway around the world alone, and had tried to talk her out of it, but Eliza had been adamant. If she didn't do it now, she probably never would. Plus, she had an uncle she had never met and at least one cousin in Picklewick, so if she could track them down she wouldn't be on her own, would she?

Eliza popped downstairs to grab her case and took it back to the bedroom, where she unpacked and dressed hastily, then she made herself some breakfast.

After a sterling meal of eggs, toast, butter and jam, washed down with two cups of tea brewed in an old-fashioned teapot with a cute horsey themed tea cosy, Eliza was ready to go exploring.

Donning a pair of sturdy boots, bought especially for the trip, and putting on a thick padded jacket with a hood, she wound a scarf around her neck, plonked a bobble hat on her head and was ready to go.

She decided she would start by walking up the lane first and see how close she could get to the farm where her dad had grown up. It irked her that she had been unable to discover who lived there now, and she wondered whether it was still in the family. Her dad's brother, Walter, had lived there up until a couple of years ago – she knew because Dad used to send a Christmas card every year – but for the past two Christmases, especially the first one without Dad, no one had felt like sending cards. For Eliza, her sister, and mum, the festive season had been a very low-key and subdued affair.

Although she was tempted to knock on the door and introduce herself, Eliza didn't feel entirely comfortable with that, so she elected to take a brisk walk-by instead. Maybe she would pop into the stables on the way back and ask for directions to Picklewick: and at the same time, she could subtly enquire whether Walter still lived there.

At the last second, Eliza dashed back inside to grab her little sketch pad, the one that fitted in her pocket, and her pencil set. One never knew when the mood might strike!

'What time do you call this?' Beth demanded as Jay staggered down the stairs and into the kitchen.

It always amazed him how sitting in an aeroplane could wear him out so much. He was knackered, as usual, and he knew it would take him a couple of days to get over the jet lag.

'Morning, Mum,' he greeted her, rather tongue-in-cheek considering it was almost noon.

'Only just. Dulcie has been up for hours. Even our Maisie managed to get up at a reasonable time.'

He scratched his beard and wished she would at least give him time to wake up properly before she started nagging. He set about making a coffee, using the flashy machine in the corner. It was a smart piece of kit and looked out of place in Dulcie's very rustic kitchen.

'Where is everyone?' he wondered.

'Dulcie and Maisie have gone into Picklewick, and Otto is at the restaurant.'

'Why didn't you go with them?' he asked, thinking that if she had, he might have had five minutes peace to get his head together.

'I wanted to see you. You're not home often.'

Drat, now he felt awful. Mum was right, though... he **hadn't** visited the UK very often these past few years, and she must miss him. He missed her too, but he had become so used to answering to no one (apart from his boss) that it was always a shock to find himself under his mother's beady and inquisitive eye.

Feeling incredibly guilty, he walked over to her and gave her a hug. She hugged him back fiercely, and he hoped she wasn't about to cry. He hated seeing her upset, and every time he left she would shed a few tears. It made him feel bad for days; but what could he do? His job used to take him to far-flung places, and

he had loved his job. He hadn't told her
that he might be home for a while, in
case he landed another contract in yet
another far-flung country, as he didn't
want to get her hopes up only to dash
them again. Thankfully she hadn't yet
twigged that he had more luggage than
usual, because it wasn't a great deal
more as he didn't own a lot, having learnt
that it was easier if he didn't have to haul
too much around every time he was
relocated.

'Tea?' he asked, and his mum nodded. He
made her a cup while his coffee brewed,
then sat down at the table with her. 'Do
you fancy showing me around the farm?'
he asked, taking a gulp of the hot liquid.

'Not on your nelly! It's bitter out there. If
you're that desperate to see it, you can

go on your own. Otherwise, you'll have to
wait for Dulcie to come back.'

Now that he had some caffeine in his
system, Jay was starting to get restless.
He wasn't used to sitting on his backside
for long periods, so he decided to take a
stroll and stretch his legs. He'd go up the
hill aways – the tarmacked lane petering
out beyond the farmyard and becoming a
dirt track – and take in the view. Dulcie
would probably want to show him around
the actual farm herself, but he was sure
she wouldn't mind if he hiked up the
mountain a bit. The fresh air would do
him good.

Leaving his mum with a crossword book
and the telly, he dressed warmly and
headed outside.

In direct contrast to yesterday, today was crisp and bright, with a weak yellow sun hanging in a pale blue sky.

Jay shivered. He wasn't used to such low temperatures and he wondered whether Dulcie was right when she'd said it would snow later in the week. He hadn't seen snow for a long time, and he felt almost as excited as Maisie – although he would never let on.

His boots ate up the ground as he made his way up the steep hill and onto the moorland above. The air was fresh, and he filled his lungs, marvelling at the crisp clean smell. It was quiet up here, too. The only noise was the wind sighing through the brown bracken and the savage call of a buzzard overhead. There weren't any insects either, and for that he was truly grateful. Buzzy flying things found him irresistible, and they irritated the hell out of him.

The hill above the farm wasn't particularly high, but the mountain seemed to roll ever upwards until he despaired of reaching the top, so when he spotted the remains of an old stone building in the distance, he gave up his quest for the top and walked towards that instead.

As it grew closer, he was able to make out that it had probably been an old farmhouse or a shepherd's hut. It was quite small, but it did have a chimney on the outside although the roof had long since gone, and he guessed it might have been rather cosy once.

The ruined, moss-covered walls looked safe enough, so he decided to go inside.

Treading carefully, he was gazing up to admire the craftsmanship that went into the stonework above the doorway, and didn't see the figure perched on a pile of rubble in the corner until it cleared its throat.

Jay let out a yell, staggered back and nearly fell.

It took him a moment to regain his balance and his equilibrium, and when he did, he realised several things simultaneously. The figure who was perched on a pile of mossy rubble was female, around his age, and very pretty.

'Sorry, I... um... didn't realise anyone would be in here,' he stuttered.

The woman gazed at him, her dark eyes inscrutable, and he wondered whether he should leave, but then she spoke.

'Am I trespassing?'

Jay thought for a second, and he recalled Dulcie saying that the land above the fields was common grazing. 'I don't believe so,' he replied, trying to get a fix on her accent.

She had only spoken three words, but he could have sworn there was a definite Antipodean twang to them. He had met loads of Kiwis and Aussies over the years, so he was fairly certain she was from that part of the world.

His gaze dropped from her face to her hands, and he saw she had a pad balanced on her knees and was holding a pencil.

'Sketching?' he hazarded a guess, scanning her face again. She had a golden tan, large eyes and plump lips that begged to be kissed. A mass of dark hair poked out from underneath a red bobble hat, fanning out over her shoulders. Long legs encased in faded jeans and ending in a pair of chunky black boots, completed the picture. God, she was cute; sexy, too, as she caught her bottom lip between her teeth.

Embarrassed to be having such thoughts and hoping they didn't show on his face, he cleared his throat.

'Yeah, I'm an artist,' she said with a shrug. From her expression he got the feeling she hadn't wanted to admit it, and he wondered if he was making her feel awkward. He was acutely aware that she was a lone female in the middle of nowhere and that she might be concerned about his presence. Perhaps he should leave and let her get on with it, but he didn't want to go, not just yet.

Trying to put her at ease, he said, 'Cool. Watercolour?'

'Mostly, but I dabble in all kinds. Whatever takes my fancy at the time.' Her eyes left him and she scanned the walls. 'Watercolour for this, I think. I love the way the stones fit together and how moss and ferns grow between the cracks. How old is it, do you know?'

Okay, so she wasn't wholly **uncomfortable** in his presence if she wanted to keep talking. He looked around and took an educated guess. 'Early last century, maybe older. Possibly nineteenth. Well over a hundred years old, I should think.'

'Crikey, I'm surprised there's anything left of it.'

'We've got way older buildings than this in the UK,' he teased.

'It's that obvious, huh?'

'That you're not from these parts? A bit. Australia?'

'New Zealand.'

'Whereabouts?'

'You won't know it – Ruakaka? It's about a hundred and thirty kilometres north of Aukland?'

He liked the way her voice lifted at the end of each sentence, so it sounded like a question. It was a common trait amongst Kiwis, and he found it endearing. On **her**, that is: not so much on his former colleagues who had all happened to be guys. He hadn't found them endearing at all.

'Have you been in the UK long?' he asked.

'I arrived last night.'

He blinked in surprise. Just a day in the country and she'd already found her way to Picklewick? He guessed she must have family or friends in the village. 'I take it you flew into Heathrow? Weren't you tempted to explore London, see the sights?'

'No, I don't like cities much. Too many people. This,' she gestured around her, 'is more my scene. I like nature.'

'So do I.' Jay beamed at her. 'I'm Jay, by the way.'

'Eliza. Nice to meet you.' She glanced down at the drawing pad and Jay took the hint.

'I'll, er, leave you to it. Nice meeting you.'

'You, too.'

He turned on his heel, but before he left, he said over his shoulder, 'Maybe I'll see you around?'

Her smile seemed genuine. 'Maybe...'

Guessing he probably wouldn't see her again, he gave her one last look, then left. But out of sight didn't mean out of mind, and she stayed in his head all the way back to the farm and then some.

CHAPTER TWO

Eliza watched the guy walk away and kept her eyes on him until he was out of sight. He'd seemed harmless enough, but he had given her a scare when he'd appeared in the doorway, and suddenly she had been acutely aware that she was on her own on this mountain and not a soul in the world knew she was here.

'Stupid, Eliza, really stupid,' she muttered, taking her mobile out of her pocket. Relieved to discover that she had a signal (Petra had been right about the coverage being patchy), Eliza pinged off a quick message to her mum and sister on the group chat to let them know she had arrived safe and sound, and that she was planning to explore the local area today. She also attached a photo of the sketch she'd just done, in the vain hope that one or the other of them might be interested.

Getting stiffly to her feet (it was too cold to be sitting on blocks of stone and she had begun to seize up), Eliza took a final look at the ruins, then retraced her steps down the hill, keeping a close eye out for Jay. The guy had seemed nice enough, but she didn't particularly want to bump into him again when she was on her own on a bleak hillside.

He was rather cute though, although cute was probably not the best way to describe him. Sexy was better, but sexy had got her into trouble in the past. Archer had been sexy. He had been a charmer, too. She had a feeling this fella might be equally as charming, so if she did happen to see him again, she would make sure to keep her distance.

There was one thing she was kicking herself for though, and that was not asking him about Lilac Tree Farm. As a local, he might have known whether Walter still lived there. Despite her internet digging, she'd not been able to determine whether or not her uncle still owned the place. Or whether he was even alive. Dad had been younger than him, and Dad had been dead for two years, so it was entirely possible that Walter had also passed away.

Eliza paused, her foot raised, slowly lowering it as a thought occurred to her. Might the fella she had just met be her cousin? She knew Walter had a son in his mid-thirties, and she estimated that the chap with the green-blue eyes was around that age.

But for some reason she hadn't got the impression Jay was a farmer. Although his light tan indicated that he spent time outdoors, he looked more like someone who had just returned from a winter holiday in the sun rather than a windswept weather-beaten farmer.

Meh, why was she wasting time thinking about him and wishing she had picked his brains, when she could pay a visit to the stables and pick the brains of someone there instead. The stables were just down the lane from the farm, so Petra must surely be able to give her some information about it.

Just as she had on the way up the mountain, Eliza slowed as she passed the entrance to the farm on her way back down, and tried not to look as though she was looking. Which was difficult, because she most definitely **was** looking, and it would be obvious to anyone who saw her.

However, despite her nosing as she sauntered past, there wasn't a soul in sight. The yard was empty of people, cars and animals, and she slowed even more as she studied it. She could just imagine her father walking across those very cobbles from the farmhouse to the barns, and she closed her eyes briefly as a wave of grief crashed over her.

Every so often it would catch her unawares, and the resulting sadness was overwhelming. Those instances were becoming less frequent and not as intense, but she suspected they would never totally leave her.

A bleating coming from inside one of the barns brought her out of her thoughts, and she gave herself a shake. It was too cold to be standing around daydreaming, and she hurried off down the lane. If she discovered that her uncle did still live on the farm, she would go and introduce herself properly. Even if he was no longer there, she might knock on the door anyway and ask if she could have a look around. The worst they could do was say no, and if she didn't ask, she wouldn't get.

The stable yard was a far different beast today to the way it had looked last night, and the doors to all the stalls were either fully open, or half-open. A couple of the half-open ones had equine heads poking over the tops, the animals' ears flicking back and forth at her approach.

She was stroking one of the soft noses when a voice said, 'Can I help you?' and she glanced around to see an elderly gentleman walking across the yard. He was carrying something wrapped in what appeared to be a red and white checked tea towel.

'Hi, my name's Eliza. I'm staying in one of the cottages.'

'Ah yes, pleased to meet you, Eliza. You met my niece last night – Petra. Is the cottage to your satisfaction?'

'It's lovely,' Eliza enthused. 'And the welcome basket was a nice touch. I've already tucked into it – eggs, bread and jam for breakfast.' She spied a chicken pecking about on the cobbles. 'I see you've got chooks, so I'm guessing the eggs are from here?'

'Name's Amos,' the old gent said. 'The eggs are indeed from our hens, and I also made the jam and the bread.' He held up the tea towel. 'I've just baked Petra a loaf, in fact.'

'It was delicious. I wish I could bake.' She hesitated, aware of his expectant expression. He was clearly wondering what she wanted. 'Petra said she would give me directions to the village,' she continued. 'I've already been up the lane for a walk. That was okay, wasn't it? There's a track just past the farm leading into the hill and I didn't see any keep-out signs.'

'You won't, either,' Amos said. 'It's a public right of way, a footpath, although not many people come walking up here in the depths of winter.'

'I was going to ask at the farm, but...'
Eliza wrinkled her nose. 'It isn't part of
the stables, is it?' Subtle, **not**, but if it got
her the answer she was looking for...

'No, it's owned by Dulcie Fairfax. You'll
probably meet her at some point. She's
about the same age as you. Nice girl.
Wants to keep goats.'

'Right. I see. Thanks. And thank Petra for
me, for the wine? It was very thoughtful.'

'I will. Now, those directions you
wanted... Go back to the old cowshed,
then—'

'Sorry, what old cowshed?' she
interrupted. Surely he didn't mean the
derelict building she had just sketched?

Amos tutted to himself. 'The cottages you
are staying in have been up over a year,

and I still refer to them as the old cowshed. It used to be a cowshed, see, until Harry – that's Petra's husband – had the idea of turning it into holiday lets.'

'Do you keep cows?' she asked. She hadn't seen any this morning, just horses in the fields below the stables and the occasional sheep on the hill.

'No, just horses. And a donkey. And two goats, but they're up at the farm with Dulcie at the moment. And chickens, of course, and a dog and a cat. This used to be a farm, many years ago when my wife's parents owned it, but not now. Mags, my wife, preferred horses. And so do I.' Amos shuddered. 'Cows get this look about them and you can't tell what they're thinking most of the time.'

A shiver travelled down Eliza's spine. Surely not, she thought; if there had been two farms on Muddypuddle Lane, maybe she had got it wrong and **this one** was the farm she was looking for? 'This used to be a **farm**?' she squeaked.

'Yes, but as I said, that was years ago.'

'It wasn't called **Lilac Tree** Farm, was it?'

'No, Lilac Tree Farm is the one further up the lane.'

Eliza sagged. 'I thought it was, but for a second there...' Amos was looking at her curiously and she knew she had to explain. 'My dad used to live there,' she said. 'Many years ago, before he emigrated to New Zealand.'

'Your **dad**? That was Walter York's old place. He lived there all his life. Your dad couldn't have—' Amos broke off, and realisation flared in his eyes. 'Walter had a **brother**, younger than him. He moved to New Zealand... You aren't... you **are**! You're Walter's niece!'

'I am!' Tears pricked at the back of Eliza's eyes. She had found someone who knew Walter. 'Do you know where he moved to? You said a woman called Dulcie owns it now.' She froze and her heart sank as her fears resurfaced. 'Is he dead?' she asked in a small voice.

'He most definitely is not.'

Relief cascaded through her. 'Can you give me his address?'

'I can go one better. I can take you to him!'

Eliza expected Amos to drive her to Walter, so she was surprised when, after he had taken the newly baked loaf into the house, Amos had ushered her out of the stables on foot, and at that point she assumed they must be walking to the village.

But when he turned left to go up the hill and came to a halt outside a small cottage about halfway between the stables and the farm, she did a double take. It had fairy lights around the porch and a Christmas wreath on the door, and her heart leapt into her mouth when Amos lifted the knocker.

Time seemed to stand still as the door slowly opened and she caught her first look at her uncle... Her breath caught in her throat, her heart thudded wildly and she must have let out a small sound, because she was aware of Amos staring at her.

She didn't look at him, though – her attention was fixed on the man standing in front of her. With a strange sense of déjà vu, and for the second time that day, Eliza was shocked by a man in a doorway. But this was no stranger: this man looked so much like her dad that it was only with great restraint Eliza didn't throw herself at him.

Walter was staring at her too, but there was only mild curiosity on his face and no recognition. How could there be when she was the spit of her mother?

Amos spoke first. 'Walter, this is Eliza York.'

Then she studied her uncle's expression as curiosity turned to bewilderment and incomprehension.

'York? I don't understand.' Walter's gaze shifted from her to Amos, and back again.

'Emrys was my father,' she said, and dawning understanding spread across his face before the colour drained from his cheeks and he grasped the doorframe for support.

Seeing him so shocked, Eliza had a terrible feeling that she had made the biggest mistake of her life in coming here. Had her dad and Walter parted on bad terms? She hadn't thought so, but who knew what had happened all those years ago? Her father had spoken about his childhood on the farm, but he had been very reticent about his latter years in the UK. And Walter's reaction convinced her that something bad must have taken place. Why else did the old chap look as though he was about to collapse?

Thankfully Amos took charge, because all Eliza could do was stand there and wish she'd stayed at home. She should have listened to her mother. Mum had told her that nothing good ever came of digging up the past. Eliza wouldn't have come if she'd realised – she had just assumed that her mum hadn't wanted her to fly halfway across the world and meet her extended family in case Eliza had liked the UK so much that she wouldn't want to come back. That very same thing had happened when a son of one of her mother's good friends had tracked down his Irish roots. Barry Skomer was now living in a tiny hamlet near Galway, fishing for lobster and crab.

Then there was the letter Eliza had found when she had been going through her dad's documents, and although it wasn't the sole reason why Eliza was here in Picklewick, it had piqued her curiosity about her dad's past before he had emigrated to New Zealand. The heartbroken reaction of Julie Richards, the woman who Eliza had contacted as per the request in her dad's letter, had made her realise just how little she knew about her father's earlier life. What had this woman been to her dad, for him to want her to be contacted and informed of his death?

Without a word, Amos hustled Walter inside and sat him down in a straight-backed armchair. A dog wandered in and lay on its master's feet, as though it knew something was amiss.

'Come in,' Amos said to her, seeing her hovering uncertainly in the tiny hall. 'Walter will be alright. It's the shock of seeing you, that's all. It's my fault, I should have warned him.'

'No, it's mine,' she replied, miserably.

'Nonsense. Put the kettle on and make him a cup of tea. Strong, mind you, none of this dishwater stuff. Milk and two sugars. Make one for yourself, too. I'll be off – I expect you've got a lot of catching up to do. Chop chop,' he added, when she didn't move.

Eliza bit her lip and sidled past the old man, heading for the expanse of gleaming steel and chrome she could see through an open door beyond the lounge. Once in the kitchen, she hunted ineffectually for the kettle, until she realised that the curved tap arching over the sink spat out boiling water as well as cold.

Seeing a teapot on a nearby benchtop, she soon found the tea bags and filled the pot with hot water. While it brewed, she searched out a couple of mugs and tried to listen to the conversation in the next room, but she couldn't make out what they were saying.

Taking the milk out of a very impressive fridge that was stocked to the rafters with all kinds of foodstuffs, she marvelled that the old gent had such an impressive kitchen, and guessed he must really love to cook. It looked more like the kitchen of a bistro she used to work in when she was a teenager, than the sort of set-up usually seen in a house as small as this.

When she returned to the lounge, a mug in each hand, she was relieved to find

Walter looking more robust. For a while, she had been terrified he was going to collapse.

'Put the mugs on the coffee table,' he instructed, and she did as she was asked, trying not to let his voice get to her; he sounded so much like her dad, it made her heart ache.

'So, you're Emrys's daughter? The eldest one?' he asked, reaching for his tea and grasping the mug with both hands to lift it to his mouth.

'Yes. I'm Eliza.'

'Are your mother and sister with you?'

'No, it's just me.'

He slurped his tea then nodded slowly, his eyes searching her face. 'You don't look much like him.'

'I take after my mum. You look like my dad, though.'

'We both followed our dad, your grandfather. In looks, that is. I was more like him in my ways, but your dad, not so much.'

'After Dad died, I wanted to see where he grew up,' she said, trying to explain why she had turned up out of the blue, unannounced. 'This is...' She grappled to find the right words. 'A kind of pilgrimage, I suppose.'

'You must miss him.' Walter had regained the colour in his cheeks, and his shocked expression had mellowed into a sympathetic one. He was gazing at her with kindly eyes.

'I do.' She bit her lip, as much to stop herself from bursting into tears as from asking Walter whether he missed his brother.

'Were you close?' Walter asked.

'Very. I was a proper daddy's girl. Cathy, my sister, is more of a mummy's girl, so we kind of had a parent each.'

'Then you lost yours?'

'Yeah...'

'How is your mother? Is she well?'

Eliza nodded. 'She misses my dad, though.'

'I expect she does.' Walter lapsed into silence and Eliza felt awkward. She should have asked Amos to alert her uncle that she was here, and not spring it on him like this. It had clearly been a big shock, but for some reason she had hoped for more emotion from him. Not gushing displays of affection as such, but **some** indication that he was pleased to see her would be nice.

'When did you sell the farm?' she asked. 'Before I arrived, I tried to find out if you were still there, but I couldn't, otherwise I'd have got in contact beforehand.'

'I moved out earlier in the year. Dulcie Fairfax owns it now.' He smiled wearily. 'It hasn't changed much since I was a boy. Dulcie's got plans for it, though.'

'Is Dulcie a relation?' she asked. She knew Walter had a son, Otto, but she hadn't heard of anyone called Dulcie until Amos mentioned her a few minutes ago.

'She's my son's girlfriend. They live together at the farm, but she owns it. It's a long story.' He paused, and she could see him struggling with something. 'Did your dad have a good life?' he blurted.

Eliza blinked. 'I think so. He seemed happy.'

Walter's smile was tinged with sadness. 'That's good. I'm glad he found love again.'

She drew in a slow breath, willing herself to stay calm. **'Again?'**

He winced. 'Ah. Right. You didn't know. That was the reason he left. Not all of it, but some of it. Mind you, he wasn't living at the farm by then, or even in Picklewick. He was living in Thornbury.' He stopped and studied her. 'Are you sure you want to hear this?'

'Yes.' Eliza was emphatic. 'I want to know all about Dad; the good and the bad.'

His expression was compassionate. 'There is plenty of good, but not much bad, you'll be pleased to hear. You mightn't believe it, but I miss him too, even though I haven't clapped eyes on him for over thirty years. It's strange to think he's gone. He was younger than me.' Without warning a huge smile lit up his face. 'I'm so happy you're here. I never thought I'd get to meet one of Emrys's daughters. We've got such a lot of catching up to do.'

He's right, Eliza thought. She and Walter had a lifetime to catch up on, so that was exactly what they did.

CHAPTER THREE

Jay was in the living room, enjoying the warmth from a hearty fire and wondering what time dinner would be, when the front door opened. He looked up from the book he was reading when he heard Otto's voice, then the sound of an older man, Walter. He had met Otto's dad when Walter joined them for dinner last night, and Jay guessed he must be eating with them again this evening.

Otto had insisted on cooking once more (he did that a lot, apparently) and Jay was looking forward to it. The meal yesterday had been exceptional, and so was the soup he'd eaten for lunch, which Otto had prepared this morning and had left on the stove so everyone could help themselves. Jay had helped himself to two portions – all that walking had given him an appetite.

His eldest sister, Nikki, had rocked up half an hour earlier with her son, Sammy, saying that Gio (her partner, who Jay had yet to meet) was working, and that she had also been invited to dinner. Jay thought it would be great having the whole family together – something that hadn't happened since last Christmas. He had seen so little of his nephew over the years, that it would be fun getting to know him. Sammy had brought his puppy with him, and Jay wondered whether Nikki would allow him to take Sammy and the dog for a walk tomorrow. He had enjoyed his hike up the hillside today, but it would have been more fun if he'd had company. Perhaps he could also persuade his sisters to come with him? If everyone carried on eating the way they had last night, they would need all the exercise they could get!

Dulcie, who had been sitting on the floor playing with Sammy and the dog, leapt to her feet as soon as she heard Otto's voice, her face glowing with happiness, and she rushed into the hall. Sammy followed her, with the pup hot on his heels, and Nikki and his mum also got up, leaving Jay alone.

He decided to remain where he was, relishing the (very) brief moment of peace. His family was rather loud, and he wasn't used to being around so many people, no matter how much he loved them, and he had to admit it was rather overwhelming. If it hadn't already been dark, he might have considered a quick stroll before dinner to recharge his depleted social battery.

An image of the ruined farmhouse on the hillside above swam into his mind, and Jay rested the book on his stomach and dropped his head back against the cushion, his thoughts filled with the woman he'd met earlier today. He had been thinking about her on and off since he'd returned to the farm, but he couldn't work out why. She had been pretty, but he had seen pretty women before. He'd even dated a few. What was so memorable about this one?

Perhaps it was because he hadn't been expecting to hear an accent like hers in Picklewick, and especially not on top of a mountain on a cold December day. It had made him feel slightly homesick for warmer climes; so much so that he could practically hear her voice in his head.

Hang on a sec... he **was** hearing her voice. Really **hearing**, not imagining!

Book forgotten, Jay leapt to his feet and went to join the rest of the family in the kitchen, where everyone had congregated.

And came face-to-face with the woman from this morning.

She was standing in his sister's kitchen and gazing around intently, then she turned her head a fraction, caught sight of him, and her intense expression turned to one of surprised recognition. 'Jay?'

'Eliza. Hi.'

Dulcie's mouth dropped open. 'Do you two know each other?'

'We met this morning,' Jay explained, a million questions flying around in his head. 'She was out for a walk and so was I.'

'Did she tell you that she's Walter's niece?' his sister asked. 'Her dad and Walter grew up on this farm.'

Eliza, who had been looking rather shell-shocked, found her voice. 'I wanted to see where Dad was born.'

That explained why she was in Picklewick, Jay thought. But he was surprised no one had mentioned her last night, and he wondered why she hadn't joined them for dinner considering Walter had been there. But perhaps that was why Walter had left as soon as he'd eaten his pudding, Jay mused, remembering that she had told him she had arrived last night.

Walter said, 'She's staying at one of the cottages at the stables. I told her she could stay with me, but Eliza is adamant she wants to remain where she is.'

'I don't blame her,' Otto laughed. 'This lot are a bit much to take in all at once, and considering you're here almost as much as you're in your own house, Dad, she'll not know what's hit her. At least she'll get a bit of peace at Petras's place.'

'Oi!' Dulcie elbowed him and Beth waved her fist. Maisie poked her tongue out as she came into the kitchen, catching the tail end of the conversation, the arrival of visitors having flushed her out of her bedroom.

Otto said to Eliza, 'See what I mean? Not only are they rowdy, but they can be violent.' He danced out of the way of jabby elbows. 'You can't hit me, I'm cooking dinner.' He laughed at Dulcie, then turned to Eliza. 'If they haven't put you off, do you still want to join us for dinner?'

She bit her lip and glanced at Walter, who nodded encouragingly. 'If that's okay?' she replied, shyly.

Otto grinned. 'Right!' He clapped his hands. 'Everyone out, unless you are keen on helping.'

There was a mad scramble for the door, Dulcie grabbing hold of Eliza's hand and tugging her out of the kitchen.

Jay watched them go, remaining where he was.

He caught Otto giving him an amused look. 'It's just me and you,' the chef said, 'and a meal for nine to prepare.'

'Er, okay.' Jay didn't mind cooking, but he wasn't terribly good at it. However, he could follow instructions and prepare veg, so as long as he left the actual cooking to Otto, it should be fine. Besides, he may as well make himself useful if he was going to stay in the kitchen and not join the others.

Raucous laughter drifted from the living room, and Jay surreptitiously nudged the kitchen door closed. He had been utterly shocked to see Eliza, and he needed time to process it, having gone from assuming he would never see her again, to eating dinner with her in the blink of an eye. To say he was surprised would be an understatement.

Otto set him to work chopping onions for a ragu sauce, while Otto made pappardelle – from scratch, no less! Jay had never heard of it; his pasta always came out of a packet and was the usual kind, such as spaghetti, tagliatelle, or the one that looked like little shells. He had once bought fresh ravioli, though...

Otto chatted whilst he worked. 'I got the shock of my life when I called into Dad's to bring him up the farm for dinner and was introduced to a long-lost cousin,' he was saying.

'Didn't you know about her?' Jay was curious.

'I kind of forgot I had any relatives in New Zealand. It has been me and Dad for such a long time. Mum died when I was in my teens,' he added. 'I remember seeing envelopes with New Zealand stamps on them at Christmas, but I honestly didn't take much notice.'

Jay said, 'She seems nice.' She seemed more than nice, if he was honest. He was quite taken with her. She was an attractive woman and one he would like to get to know better.

He hoped she would be around for a while, because if she was, the relaxing Christmas he had been anticipating was about to get a lot more exciting.

Eliza had assumed that the stranger on the hill was a local, but she hadn't expected to see him in the farm's kitchen this evening.

Confused as to who all these people were (when Walter's son, Otto, had arrived at Walter's house to take him to dinner at the farm, she had expected to share the meal with just Walter, Otto and Dulcie)

Eliza been taken aback when faced with three women, a boy of around twelve or thirteen, plus a puppy who had bounded around like an idiot until Walter's dog Peg had told it off by growling at it. Then Jay had put in an appearance, as well as a fourth woman, and Eliza had been completely thrown.

So many questions were whirling around in her head. Was he married to one of the women? Which one was Dulcie? Who was the older woman? Dulcie's mother? Not Otto's, because she knew that his mum – her aunt – had died years ago. Or was she Jay's mum?

Walter came to her rescue after Dulcie had dragged her into a spacious sitting room and gestured for her to take a seat. Eliza sank into the squashy armchair, feeling somewhat overwhelmed.

'Let me introduce you to everyone. This is Dulcie.' Walter gave one of the women a squeeze. 'She's Otto's girlfriend, and she owns the farm. This is Nikki and her son Sammy. Nikki is Dulcie's older sister, and the other one is Maisie, the baby of the family. This lovely lady is Beth, their mother. And you've already met Jay.'

Eliza had, but all he had told her was his name – and she was still none the wiser as to which sister he belonged to, Nikki or Maisie.

'You must tell us all about your life down under,' Dulcie said.

'What do you want to know?' Eliza asked uncertainly.

'Leave her be,' Walter leapt in. 'She doesn't leave until the second of January,

so you'll have plenty of time to quiz her.
Let her get used to you first.'

'It's okay,' Eliza said, but she was glad
he'd intervened. She still couldn't believe
she was sitting in the same room which
her father had sat in all those years ago,
and she wondered if it had changed
much.

With the room full of people and dogs, it
was hard to envisage him here. If it had
just been her and Walter, she might have
found it easier. But the farm didn't belong
to her uncle anymore and she could
hardly ask everyone to leave just so she
could soak up the atmosphere of the past.

'Stop being a fusspot, Walter,' Beth, the
oldest of the four women, said. 'You make
us sound scary.'

'If the cap fits...' Walter muttered.

'I heard that!' Beth was indignant.

'You were meant to.'

'Take that back.'

Walter stuck his tongue out at her, and Eliza burst out laughing.

'Don't take his side,' Beth warned. 'Blood isn't always thicker than water – not if you want any dinner.'

'Mum, stop it.' Nikki frowned at her mother, then turned to Eliza. 'She isn't always like this.'

'Yes, she is,' Walter retorted. 'She's a right pain in the ar—'

'Walter!' Dulcie cried. 'Why do you act like a pair of kids every time you're in the same room?'

'I behaved myself yesterday,' Beth objected.

'So did I.' That was from Walter. 'I was as nice as pie at dinner.'

'Only because you ate and ran,' Beth snapped. 'He gobbled his meal down then buggered off home.'

'That's because there's only a certain amount of you I can take.'

'Well!' Beth pressed her lips together and folded her arms across her chest, her expression stony.

'If you can't play nice, **neither** of you will have any dinner,' Nikki said in a commanding voice.

Walter leant towards Eliza and hissed, 'Spot the primary school teacher.'

'Nikki?' she guessed.

'Got it in one. I wonder if she speaks to Gio like a naughty schoolboy when he does something she doesn't like.'

'Gio?'

'Her other half. He's a copper. They've got a house in the village.'

Ah, so Jay must be with Maisie, Eliza concluded. But as her gaze slid across Maisie's face, she couldn't see those two as a couple for some reason, even though they would look good together.

All three sisters were attractive women. They had got their looks from their mother, she realised. Despite her grumpy demeanour and downturned mouth, Beth had good cheekbones and lovely blue-green eyes. Jay had nice blue-green eyes too—

Eliza's mouth dropped open as a thought struck her. Quickly closing it again and hoping no one had spotted her gormless expression, Eliza shuffled closer to Walter and said out of the corner of her mouth, 'Is Jay Beth's son?'

Walter blinked. 'Yes, why?'

'No reason, just trying to get everyone straight in my head. Are there any other brothers or sisters I should know about?' she asked lightly.

'Why are you two whispering?' Beth demanded. 'It's rude to whisper.'

'I was just explaining to my niece—' he puffed out his chest at the word '—that Jay is your son. The poor boy.'

Beth glared at him, and Dulcie rolled her eyes.

'Dulcie is getting goats tomorrow,' Sammy announced. The child had been sitting on the floor playing with the puppy, but he suddenly leapt to his feet, put his index fingers to his head like horns and began bleating.

'Stop being silly, Sammy,' his mother said, and the boy subsided.

'Do they have goats in New Zealand?' he asked Eliza. 'I like goats.'

'So do I.' That was from Maisie – the first words Eliza had heard the woman speak. Until now, she had been focused on her phone, her thumbs flying across the screen.

'Yes, there are goats in New Zealand,'
Eliza said with a smile. 'And sheep.'

'Aunty Dulcie hates sheep,' Sammy
sniggered. 'Otto had to rescue her from
Flossie. Dulcie was hiding in the house,
screaming that it was going to eat her.'

'Flossie is a sheep,' Walter explained.
'She's as tame as my dog, Peg. I hand
reared her, you see.'

'I was not screaming,' Dulcie objected.

'Uncle Otto said you were.' Sammy
sniggered again.

'Uncle Otto was exaggerating.'

'What was I exaggerating about?' Otto
asked. His head had appeared around the
living room door, and he brought with him
the enticing smell of cooking. Eliza's
tummy rumbled.

'Flossie,' Sammy and Maisie chorused.

Otto grinned, and said to Eliza, 'Have they been telling you about sheepgate? You wait until you hear how she screeched when she came face-to-face with her first chicken. It was so loud that the dogs in the next county must have heard.'

Dulcie huffed. 'How long is dinner going to be?'

'It's ready, my sweet, so if everyone would like to take their seats? Jay has laid the table. Eliza, I believe you will be sitting between him and Walter.' He winked at her, and Eliza wondered what that was about.

Apprehensively, she followed Walter into the dining room and sat beside him. The chair to her right was empty, but not for long, as Jay slipped into it. He was so close she could smell his cologne. The scent made the hairs on her arms stand on end.

Otto came in holding huge bowls of steaming pasta in each hand and placed them on the table. Baskets of bread, a block of Parmesan cheese and a jug of water already graced the table, and after Otto had hurried into the kitchen once more, returning with a bowl of rich red sauce and a ladle, everyone began reaching for everything at once, all of them talking at the same time.

Except for her and Jay.

Like her, Jay seemed to be waiting for the rush to abate. 'Can I pour you a glass of water?'

'Please.'

'Can I have wine?' Maisie asked.

'No,' Dulcie and Otto chorused at the same time.

Maisi pouted. 'Why not? We had wine with dinner last night.'

Jay moved one of the bowls of pasta towards Eliza and began to lift some onto her plate. 'Say when,' he told her.

'Because we drank it all,' Dulcie said. 'I'm going to have to go to the supermarket tomorrow and stock up for Christmas.'

'Can you get me a bottle of sherry?' Beth asked. 'Actually, make that two.'

'When,' Eliza said to Jay, then he ladled a large spoonful of sauce on top of her pasta, before he served himself.

'I like Prosecco,' Maisie said.

'I want beer.' This was from Sammy, and the table fell silent as everyone turned to look at him. 'What?' he asked, his chin covered in red sauce.

Eliza could see Jay struggling to hold in his mirth, and Otto was also trying not to smile.

'You're not having beer.' Sammy's mother was adamant.

Eliza ate a mouthful of pasta and almost swooned in delight. The sauce was rich and fragrant, and she thought it was the best she had ever tasted. No wonder Otto was opening his own restaurant. Walter had been so full of pride when he'd told her about his son, and she could understand why. The man was a genius in the kitchen if he could make a simple meal like pasta with tomato sauce taste so divine.

Sammy was pouting. 'You're mean.'

Nikki said, 'Yep, mean is my middle name. You are too young to drink beer. Or any other kind of alcohol, for that matter.'

Eliza mentally gave her a high five for cutting any further alcohol-related requests from her son off at the pass.

'Aunty Maisie does, and you said she's a big kid,' Sammy replied.

Silence descended once more, but this time there was no humour in it.

Nikki shook her head and glared at her son, who gazed back at her innocently. Beth was tutting, and Dulcie's head was down as she concentrated on her food.

'Is that what you think of me?' Maisie asked eventually. Her jaw was hard and her eyes flashed.

With a shake of her head at Sammy, a clear warning that she would deal with him later, Nikki replied, 'If you want the truth, yes. You flit from job to job, from boyfriend to boyfriend, and you expect Mum to do your washing and ironing, to cook you a meal every evening, and to clean up after you... If that's not behaving like a teenager, I don't know what is.'

Maisie gasped, before rallying. 'It's better than being uptight. You act like you've got a broom stuck up your backside and a face like a slapped—'

'That's enough!' Beth smacked her palm down on the table, making everyone jump and the glasses rattle. 'May I remind you we have a guest? What must she think of us? Sorry, Eliza, we're not normally like this.'

'Yes, they are,' Jay whispered in her ear, once everyone had resumed eating.

'They?' she whispered back. 'Don't you include yourself?'

'My sisters fight like ferrets in a bag. I'm sweetness and light.' He assumed an exaggeratedly virtuous expression, then sobered. 'I hope we haven't scared you off?'

'Only a bit,' she replied, smiling to show she didn't mean it.

She had to admit to being a little taken aback, though – her own family were considerably more subdued than this one. If she was feeling unkind, she might even say they were repressed. She loved her mother to pieces, but Mum would often sulk if she didn't get her own way, and if she didn't approve of something, she had a habit of giving whoever it was who had upset her the silent treatment. Out of herself and her sister, Eliza was often on the receiving end of that. It was an eye-opener to see the way this family dealt with their issues, and she wasn't sure which method she preferred.

Thankfully the little spat was soon forgotten and Eliza carried on eating her meal, quietly observing the family, but at the same time acutely aware of the man sitting beside her.

He didn't say a lot either, but now and again he would smile indulgently as the conversation swirled around them.

'So, Eliza,' Dulcie said, 'I'm dying of curiosity here. Is this your first visit to the UK?'

Eliza hastily swallowed a mouthful of food and nodded. 'It is.'

'And you go back on the second of January, is that right?'

'Yes. I'm here for two weeks.'

'When did you arrive?'

'Yesterday.'

Jay said, 'I only arrived myself last night.'

'Ah, yes, you two have already met.' Dulcie's gaze darted between them, before coming back to rest on Eliza.

Eliza felt the need to explain. 'I was out for a walk and was exploring this derelict building on the top of the hill, when I saw Jay.'

'She was inside, sketching,' Jay said. 'I think I gave her the fright of her life when I appeared in the doorway.'

'I think you were equally as surprised,' she said, remembering the way he'd almost jumped out of his skin.

'Are you an artist?' This was from Maisie.

'I am.' Eliza blushed self-consciously. She had always found it difficult to acknowledge that she earned a living from her creativity, even when her dad had been alive. Only having one person out of the family who believed in her, had made her hesitant about telling people.

'Are you online? Do you have an Instagram page?' Maisie asked, reaching for the phone next to her plate.

'I am and I do,' Eliza admitted.

'Oh, no, you don't, Maisie Fairfax,' Beth interjected. 'Put your phone down and don't be rude. You can play on it later, after we've eaten.' Beth turned to Eliza and said, 'If I had my way, I'd ban mobiles from the table.'

Maisie protested, 'I was just—'

'Shush.' Her mother arched her eyebrows and Maisie subsided, grumbling under her breath.

'Eliza is very talented,' Walter said, his voice oozing with pride. 'She showed me some of her paintings.'

And at that, Eliza felt a spark reignite in her heart – a spark she thought had been extinguished when her dad died. Would Walter be her new champion? God knows she needed one; her mother certainly wasn't, and her sister couldn't care less.

'Eliza takes after **my** mother, her grandmother,' Walter was saying. 'She also liked to sketch and paint. The picture above my fireplace is one that she did.'

'You never said,' Dulcie chimed in. 'I assumed you'd had it commissioned. It's lovely.'

Eliza hadn't known what to feel when Walter showed it to her earlier. Her dad had spoken about his mother's artistic streak with fondness, but to see something her grandmother had painted had brought a lump to her throat.

'My niece is just as good... better, I think,' he said, as Eliza's blush deepened.

And her face was positively on fire when Jay leant closer (so close that she could smell his clean-skin scent, with a light overlay of cologne) and said softly, 'Take the compliment.'

'You don't understand,' she murmured, without thinking, and wished she could take the words back when she sensed his curiosity.

'Perhaps you could explain it to me sometime?'

'Maybe.' Eliza was just being polite – she had no intention of sharing anything with a man she'd only just met. She might tell Walter, but it was honestly no biggie: all families had their issues, and her mum and sister not believing in her talent was hardly a major one. Besides, she had proved them wrong, to a point. She **was** supporting herself through her art, although it hadn't made her rich yet and probably never would.

But seeing the way this rambunctious family argued and squabbled one minute, then made up and were the best of friends the next, made her wonder whether she had been blowing things out of all proportion. Maybe her mum's opinion didn't matter as much as she thought it did.

She'd call home tomorrow, she decided. She would take a stroll into the village – she needed some groceries – and give her a bell. Mindful of the thirteen-hour time difference, as long as she didn't leave it too late, she would hopefully catch her mum before she went to bed.

Dessert followed (a wonderful molten chocolate cake) and as they finished the meal, Eliza continued to be quizzed about where she lived, what life was like 'down under' and about her family. Although she felt bombarded, their interest was friendly and she enjoyed telling them about her homeland.

Finally, after a sumptuous cheeseboard, she was stuffed, and jetlag was catching up with her.

It seemed to be catching up with Jay too, and she smiled when she caught his eye mid-yawn. Over the course of the meal, she'd found out that the tan she had noticed earlier had been acquired in Borneo, and that he worked for an organisation which installed and monitored acoustic listening devices in the jungle. It sounded fascinating and she would have liked to have learnt more, but the conversation never seemed to linger on any one subject for long.

By the time everyone retired to the lounge with cups of tea and coffee, Eliza was bushed. She was definitely all peopled-out, and she needed sleep and time to mull over the events of the day.

'Sorry, guys,' she said, after having her offer to help clear away the dinner things turned down. 'I think I'll have to call it a night. I'm exhausted.'

'I'll walk you down the hill,' Walter said, but Eliza refused.

'You stay here and enjoy the rest of the evening,' she told him. It was only eight-thirty, and she didn't want to spoil his night.

'I don't like the idea of you walking back to the stables in the dark,' Walter said, attempting to heave himself out of his chair.

Jay waved him down. 'I'll walk her home,' he said. 'I could do with stretching my legs before I hit the sack.'

Eliza said, 'It's fine, honestly. I'll be okay.'

'No doubt you will,' Walter agreed, 'but humour an old man, eh? Dulcie, have you got a torch Jay can borrow?'

'Of course.' Dulcie went to fetch one and when she returned with it, she said to Eliza, 'Would you like to pop up to the farm tomorrow and have a proper look around? About twelvish?'

'That's very kind, thank you.' Eliza was touched by the woman's thoughtfulness.

With goodbyes said, along with a promise to call in and see Walter soon, she donned her coat and headed outside. The sudden drop in temperature made her shiver, but the cessation of noise was very welcome.

'Thank goodness for some peace and quiet,' Jay said. 'I love my family to bits, but they ain't half noisy.'

'They're lovely,' Eliza said honestly. 'Look, you don't have to walk me down the hill if you don't want to.'

'I want to, and I need to get some fresh air. I just wish it wasn't quite so fresh. I forget how chilly British winters can be.'

Eliza wrapped her scarf more firmly around her neck. 'It doesn't get cold where I live – not like this.'

'It's a shock to the system, isn't it? I'm hoping we get some snow, though. It's forecast for later this week.'

'Will we get snowed in?' she asked, suddenly mindful that Muddypuddle Lane was off the beaten track.

'Possibly. Otto says that the farm has been cut off in the past.' Jay aimed the torch's beam at the ground, and she was grateful for the light. Those potholes were lethal.

'I'd better get some provisions in,' she said. 'I was planning on going to Picklewick in the morning anyway. Do you know how to get to it from here?'

'Down the lane, turn right and follow the road into the village. It's about a five-minute drive, if that.'

'I won't be driving, I'll be walking. I haven't got a car.' She should definitely think about hiring one, and she wondered where the nearest car hire centre was –

Thornbury, maybe? Or further afield? Or had she left it a bit late, considering Saturday was Christmas Day, and today was Tuesday?

'Do you need to buy much?' Jay asked.

'Some,' she admitted, wondering how she was going to carry everything back.

'I'll drive you.'

'That's kind of you, but I don't want to put you out.'

'You're not. I haven't got anything planned. Which one is yours?' he asked, as they approached the row of three little cottages.

'The middle one.' Eliza halted. 'Thanks for walking me back.' Did he expect to be invited in, she wondered in alarm.

'It's no bother.' He turned away, then said, 'What time do you want me to pick you up in the morning?'

'Is eight-thirty too early? I'd like to give my mum a call and the signal here is dire.'

'No problem. See you tomorrow. G'night.'

'Night,' she said, letting herself in, but she waited until the light from the torch had disappeared before closing the door.

What a day, she thought, as she got ready for bed. She'd met her uncle and her cousin, had eaten a meal in the very house where her dad had grown up, and had been assimilated into a family she had only just met.

And then there was Jay.

Better not think about him too much, no matter how attracted she might be, she told herself, climbing into bed. If she wasn't careful, she might land in a whole heap of trouble, because she didn't think she had imagined that he was as equally attracted to her.

CHAPTER FOUR

The following morning, Jay was far more eager than he should have been when he drove down the lane towards the stables to collect Eliza. He had tried telling himself he was simply doing a friend of the family a favour, and that this was nothing more than a quick trip into the village to pick up some groceries, but he had been telling himself that since he left her at her cottage last night and it hadn't made an iota of difference – his stomach still turned over every time he thought of her.

It continued to do somersaults as he pulled into the little parking area just up

from the row of cottages and saw her
hurrying outside to meet him.

Bloody hell, she was gorgeous, he thought
again, and a bolt of sheer lust jabbed him
in the chest, making his heart skip a beat.

Maybe offering to drive her into
Picklewick wasn't such a good idea after
all, not if he was going to react like this
every time he clapped eyes on her. But
he'd offered now and could hardly retract
it considering she was opening the car
door and getting in.

'Thanks for this,' she said. She sounded
slightly breathless, as though she'd been
rushing around, and perhaps she had.
Like him, she was probably still suffering
from jet lag, but unlike him she might
have actually had some sleep last night.
For some reason, he hadn't been able to
drop off, despite being so tired he would

have thought he could have fallen asleep on a bed of nails. Instead, he'd tossed and turned for ages, and then when he had finally managed to get some rest, he'd woken far too early. He blamed it on the blasted cockerel, who seemed to have taken a liking to the spot directly beneath his bedroom window to announce the start of a new day.

Jay was sure he looked as rough as he felt.

Eliza, on the other hand, looked as fresh as a proverbial daisy, and he guessed (rather enviously) that she must have had at least eight hours of blissful slumber.

The journey to the village took less than five minutes, and soon they were driving along a road with houses on either side.

Jay glanced around curiously. It was picture-postcard lovely, and he could see why his sister had fallen in love with the place. **Two** of his sisters actually, because Nikki had moved to the village a few months after Dulcie. Mind you, she had also fallen in love with a local chap, so that might have had something to do with it.

The main street was quaint and old-fashioned, and looked like a scene out of **A Christmas Carol**, minus the snow. Every shop window sported trees laden with baubles, reindeer, and beautifully wrapped presents, and there were festive lights draped across the lamp-posts high above. If it looked pretty now, it would look even lovelier when it was dark and all those fairy lights came to life.

'Do you mind if we go for a coffee first, so I can phone my mum?' Eliza asked. 'Or if you've got things to do, we can arrange to meet somewhere?'

'I could murder a coffee, so I'll come with you, if that's alright,' he said. 'If you don't want me listening in, we can sit at separate tables.'

She shot him a look. 'I don't mind. You'll be bored to death, though.' She caught her lip between her teeth, and he had a mad urge to kiss her.

Shaking his head at his stupidity, he concentrated on finding somewhere to park, which proved to be more difficult than he thought; but he caught lucky when a police car pulled away from the kerb and Jay shot into the resulting space. Handily, it was directly in front of a café.

Once inside, he lingered over placing their order to allow Eliza to make her call, but she was still on the phone when he carried the tray to the table where she was sitting.

Eliza smiled her thanks as he placed a mug of coffee in front of her, and as he sipped his, he scrolled through a news channel on his phone and tried not to listen to her conversation.

'You'd like it, Mum,' Eliza was saying. 'I wish you were here... It's quaint... Yeah, really small, but it's got everything I need. Did you get the sketch? I sent it to you yesterday. No...? Check your— never mind... Walter sends his regards. He looks so much like Dad. Sounds like him, too. Otto is nice... Yeah, I will. As I said, the signal is poor. Give my love to Cathy... Hmm... Right. I'll ring you when I can.

Love you, Mum.' Eliza ended the call, took a sip of her coffee, and said, 'That was my mother.'

'I thought as much.'

'She didn't want to come on this trip, but I wish she had.'

Jay, selfishly, was pleased Eliza's mother hadn't, because if she had, he probably wouldn't be sitting here with Eliza right now. Then he felt awful for putting himself before what was best for Eliza. She was clearly missing her mum and was no doubt homesick – not ideal at the best of times, but worse around the festive season.

Vowing to try to make her feel as included as possible, he made a mental note to ask Dulcie to invite Eliza for Christmas lunch. Walter was coming to them for the day anyway, so Dulcie would most likely have already thought of inviting Eliza, but just in case she hadn't, he would mention it.

'I'm hungry,' she announced. 'Can I treat you to one of those famed English breakfasts as a thank you for bringing me shopping?'

Jay beamed. 'You can. But only on the understanding that I buy the next one.'

'Will there be a next one?'

'I don't see why not. You'll probably have to go shopping more than once. And while we're here, do you think you can help me pick out some gifts for my daft family? I've brought a few things with me from Borneo, but I need some more. Take Sammy, for instance – what do you get a twelve-year-old boy for Christmas?'

'Don't look at me, I haven't got a clue. I don't have much to do with kids. Cathy, my sister, is pregnant with her first, so I dare say I'll find out in due course.'

'That's nice. Are you and she close?'

'Not really. She doesn't approve of me.'

Jay was taken aback. What was there not to approve of?

When he raised his eyebrows, Eliza said, 'I live in a bach on the beach.' She pulled a face. 'It isn't up to her or Mum's standards, but it's mine, I own it outright and I love it.'

Jay heard the defensiveness in her voice. 'What is a... what did you call it... a **batch?**'

'Yeah, it's spelt b-a-c-h,' she spelt it out, 'but it's pronounced **batch**, rhyming with hatch. They are what us Kiwis call holiday homes, and are usually near a beach or lake, or even in the forest. Mine's on the beach.'

'It sounds idyllic.'

'The setting is – the bach not so much. When I told Mum I was planning on buying one, she had visions of something a bit more upmarket; the sort of property that well-off people buy as a second home. Not the wooden shack I live in. The light is fantastic, though.'

'Do you have a studio?'

She nodded. 'It's built on the side of the house, with views of the ocean and scrubland all around. It's so calm and peaceful.'

'I can imagine.'

Eliza stared at him. Yeah, he probably could. 'What about you? Where do you live?' she asked, and over breakfast Jay told her about the rather rustic accommodation that used to be his base in Borneo, and how he had been moving around quite a bit over the years, installing acoustic sensors and training people how to use and maintain them.

'I love being outdoors,' he said. 'I love exploring and seeing the wildlife.'

'Me, too. Wildlife and landscapes are my two favourite things to paint, the sea especially.'

'Would you show me some of your work?' he asked, and when he saw how talented she was, he let out a low whistle. 'Walter said you were good, and he wasn't exaggerating.'

Her use of colour was extraordinary, and he could see why she loved painting seascapes – she was incredibly good at them. Then he came across the drawing she'd done of the ruins above the farm, and he smiled.

'I was hoping to see the end result,' he said.

'It's not finished. It's only a rough sketch.'

'It looks finished to me. Have you brought any paints with you?'

'Some, but I couldn't bring much. Just a small watercolour palette and a few brushes. Don't tell Petra, but I'm going to use her wooden chopping board to stretch my paper.'

Jay was puzzled for a moment, then he recalled his school art classes. 'That's when you pre-wet the paper and stretch it out to let it dry before you paint on it, isn't it?'

'That's right. If you don't prepare paper properly, it tends to ripple. Do you paint?'

'Nah, was hopeless at it. Can't draw either, but I can whittle.'

Eliza was laughing. 'Whittle?'

'You know, carve bits of wood.'

'What do you carve?'

'Animals, mostly.'

'Got any photos?'

'I might have.'

'Can I see?'

Jay found one on his phone and showed it to her.

'What is it?' she asked.

'It's a tapir.' He saw her blank expression. 'A creature from South America that looks a bit like a large pig, but isn't.'

'Sorry,' she said, with a pained expression. 'I don't mean to diss your tapir, but I don't know what a tapir is supposed to look like.'

Jay scrolled through his phone for another photo. 'How about this?'

'Ah, that I **do** recognise. It's an Indian elephant.'

'Thank goodness for that!' he chuckled.

'You're good,' she said.

Jay shrugged. He didn't think he was that good, but he enjoyed doing it, and that was all that mattered. Seeing that they'd finished their meal, he said, 'Shall we make a move?'

As they made their way outside and into the bitter December air, Jay shoved his hands into his coat pockets. He'd had to borrow it from Otto, because any winter gear he owned was at his mother's house in Birmingham. Luckily, he and Otto were of a similar build, although Jay was a little leaner, so the coat fitted just fine.

Speak of the devil – there was the man in question. Otto was heading into a building on the opposite side of the road, and Jay pointed him out to Eliza.

'That's where Otto is opening his restaurant,' he said.

'That's The Wild Side?'

'Yeah; has Walter told you Otto specialises in foraged ingredients?'

She nodded, her eyes on the restaurant. 'He also told me he's got a book deal. I'm not surprised – the meal he cooked last night was delicious.'

'It was, wasn't it? If he keeps feeding me like that, I'll be ten kilos heavier by the time I leave,' Jay joked. He glanced over at Eliza to find her studying the street.

She said, 'Picklewick is so pretty – exactly what I imagined a typical English village to look like. And it's so Christmassy.' Her eyes roamed over the shops. 'Gift shopping first, grocery shopping last?'

The tip of her nose had turned pink, and for a moment Jay imagined kissing it. He coughed to cover his embarrassment at having such thoughts. 'Er, okay. I'm easy.'

'Let's try here.' Eliza pushed open the door of the nearest shop and an old-fashioned bell tinkled above their heads.

It was warm and cosy inside, and smelt of waxed candles and cinnamon. Fairy lights were festooned along the shelves and carols played softly in the background. The interior of the shop was a jewel box of gold, silver, red and green, with a smattering of other colours thrown in.

'I don't think they'll have anything here for Sammy,' Eliza said, 'but who else do you need to buy for?'

You, he thought, as a vision of her on her own on Christmas morning without even a single present to open, swam into his head.

He shelved the thought for consideration later, but he couldn't help making a note of anything that caught her eye.

Eliza wandered around the shop, picking things up and putting them down again, but not lingering on any specific item. 'You say you've already bought a few things – so who do you need to buy for today?' she asked again, gazing at him expectantly.

'I've got Mum's and Maisie's gifts sorted, and a little something for Otto – authentic Asian spices – but Dulcie isn't easy to buy for, and neither is Nikki. Then there's Sammy, as I said, plus Walter and Gio.' **And you**, the voice in his head repeated.

'Let's start with Dulcie. What sort of thing does she like?'

'If you had asked me that question last Christmas, I'd have said anything sparkly and girly, but since she won the farm—'

'Excuse me,' Eliza interjected. 'Did you just say **won the farm**?'

Jay laughed. Her expression was kitten-cute. 'I did. It's a long story to do with Walter not being able to cope and running into some financial difficulties, but the result was that the farm was kind of raffled off, and Dulcie won it.'

'Blinking heck!'

'I know, right? It's unbelievable. I would never have put 'my sister' and 'owning a farm' in the same sentence, yet eight months on, she's not only loving rural life, she's trying to make a go of it.'

'So that's why Otto was teasing her about sheep and chickens? I did wonder.'

'Until she won the farm, the nearest she'd come to a chicken was a McNugget,' Jay said wryly.

'And now she's buying goats?'

'Wild, isn't it? Good luck to her, I say. She's found her niche.' **And she's found Otto**, he thought, but didn't say, not wanting to sound cheesy. But he hadn't been able to help notice how in love his sister and her man were, and if jealousy was a green-eyed monster, envy must be its emerald cousin because Jay abruptly realised that someday he hoped to have what they had.

That was the second time since he'd arrived in Picklewick that he'd had that thought, and he found it troubling.

'Essential oils!' Eliza cried, startling him.

'You what?'

'For Dulcie, for her soap making. There's a gift box here with lots of different scents. She's probably already got some, but she mightn't have all of them.'

Jay took the box of oils from her and examined it. 'Perfect. Now for Nikki.'

'I know I've only met her once, and I haven't met Gio at all, but what about something they can do together? Like a couple's spa day, or theatre tickets?'

'You're a genius. I'll have a look online later. So that just leaves Sammy and Walter.'

'I might have an idea about Sammy's present,' she said. 'Why don't you whittle him a dog? As for Walter...' Eliza shrugged.

Jay was impressed with the suggestion. 'That's a brilliant idea! I'll have to pull my finger out and get a move on, but it might be doable in two days. There's bound to be a suitable piece of wood in the huge log store in the barn.' His excitement mounting, he said, 'I'll take a look as soon as I get back.' He didn't have a clue what to get Walter though, so he said, 'I'll ask Otto about Walter. Let me pay for this, and I'm done.' He indicated the box in his hand.

That was painless, he thought. He generally disliked gift buying, but this had been enjoyable – possibly because it had been quick, and definitely because Eliza was with him. And he was looking forward to doing some whittling, too.

But as he accompanied her around the village whilst she bought her groceries, he realised he was enjoying this little shopping trip far too much, and considering Eliza would be leaving in a couple of weeks, that wasn't good, was it?

Eliza hadn't expected to see the whole of Jay's family, plus several people who worked at the stables, to be there for the Grand Goat Delivery (as she had begun to think of it) later that day. The only person missing was Otto, who she suspected was still at the restaurant. She and Jay had spotted him going into The Wild Side earlier, but they hadn't tried to attract his attention because he'd looked rather preoccupied.

After being introduced to Gio (Nikki's other half), Harry (Petra's husband), a woman about her own age who worked at the stables (but Eliza couldn't for the life of her remember her name), and Amos's partner, Eliza retreated to the back of the crowd and waited for the goats to arrive.

Dulcie and her mum were making an occasion out of it, and had made mugs of hot chocolate for everyone, and were now handing out Christmas cookies that Otto had baked. They were delicious and Eliza wondered whether she could filch another.

Glancing around in the hope of seeing an unattended plate of the gorgeous goodies, she caught Jay's eye and her own widened at the fleeting expression on his face. She could have sworn she spotted desire there, but it was swiftly replaced by a friendly smile.

'Jay seems nice,' Walter said, and she turned to see her uncle standing at her elbow. He was clutching a mug of steaming hot chocolate in one hand and a cookie in the other.

Eliza eyed it enviously. 'Yeah, he does,' she agreed. 'He gave me a lift into the village this morning.'

'So I heard.'

She shot him a keen glance. 'Who told you?'

Walter tapped the side of his nose. 'Never you mind. But what you may want to mind, is that you can't keep anything secret around here. This lot,' he jerked his head towards Beth and her daughters, 'are worse than four old biddies nattering over a garden fence.'

'I've got nothing to hide,' Eliza said with a chuckle, but she was a little ruffled to discover that Walter knew about her trip to the village, and she wondered whether he felt put out that she hadn't asked him for a lift instead.

'Did you get what you wanted?' he asked.

Eliza had got slightly **more** than she'd bargained for, namely an increased liking of, and attraction to Jay. Not only was he good-looking, but he was also fun to be with and easy to talk to, and warning bells kept going off in her head. A quick jump in the sack wasn't her cup of tea, but considering that this was all it could be, she wasn't prepared to allow anything to develop between them.

She forced herself to look anywhere except at Jay, and saw Dulcie heading their way, as she replied, 'I did, thanks. I might have to pop back for some bread and milk later in the week, but for now I'm good.'

'I hope you've not bought a turkey,' Dulcie warned, drawing alongside.

Eliza hadn't. Not even a breast of one. She would have steak and veggies instead.

When she shook her head, Dulcie said, 'Good, because you're officially invited to Lilac Tree Farm for Christmas dinner.'

'I couldn't possibly impose—' she began, but Dulcie cut her off.

'It's either that, or we come to you, and as I don't think we would all fit into your little cottage, I think it's best if you come to the farm.'

Eliza glanced at Walter, who held up his hands. 'Don't look at me,' he said. 'This isn't my doing – although I was going to ask Dulcie if she minded you joining us.'

'Jay suggested it,' Dulcie said. 'But I was going to invite you anyway.'

Eliza's gaze shot to Jay. He had his back to her, but for some reason she had a feeling he knew what was going down.

'You can't be on your own at Christmas,' Dulcie argued. 'You've come all this way to discover your roots, so whether you like it or not, you are part of our family now.'

'If you insist,' Eliza replied weakly, but deep down she was thrilled to be asked. If she was honest, she hadn't been looking forward to spending Christmas Day on her own, and it wasn't as though she could have video-called her mum to eat a festive lunch together and pretend they were in the same room. Her mum would be eating lunch at three in the morning UK time! Maybe they could open their presents at the same time though, she thought – then she remembered the abysmal phone reception, so that wouldn't work either, unless she wanted to stand on top of the hillside to open the gift her mother had thrust into her hands before she'd departed.

Gifts!

Maybe she should buy Walter something, now that she was going to be seeing him on Christmas Day. And what about everyone else? Should she get the others a little present, too?

'Good, that's sorted,' Dulcie said decisively. 'Oh, and we're off to the pub tonight, if you'd like to join us.'

Before Eliza could reply, a shout went up and she heard the sound of an engine labouring up the lane. A minute later, a truck lumbered into the yard and she saw several furry little noses poking through the bars of the trailer it was pulling. Goats were cute, and she was looking forward to seeing them, and maybe even stroking a couple of those sweet noses.

She hung back whilst the truck manoeuvred the trailer into position in front of the barn, and watched as barriers were erected to make sure the creatures went where they were meant to go.

The bleating emanating from the trailer was incessant. Eliza guessed that the animals were eager to get out, and she craned her neck to see as a collective 'Ah!' went up.

When she spotted the littlest pygmy goat tiptoeing delicately down the trailer's ramp, Eliza realised why. It was the cutest, sweetest, most adorable creature, and she had a sudden urge to paint it. Whipping out her phone, she edged closer to get a couple of photos, but as she did so, she noticed the rapture on Maisie's face.

Maisie looked like she was in love – with a goat, no less!

If Eliza hadn't already had the urge to paint, the young woman's expression would have had her reaching for her brushes in an instant.

Then Eliza smiled – she knew exactly what she was going to give this new family of hers for Christmas.

Eliza put the finishing touches to her make-up and took a look at herself in the mirror.

She'd do, she decided. Not too much slap that she looked like she was trying too hard, but enough to show that she was making an effort. She had also tried not to wear every item of clothing she had brought with her, even though it was freezing outside and getting colder by the hour.

Before she'd left the farm this afternoon (after taking what felt like hundreds of photos of the goats and several of Maisie – without the woman's knowledge, but

Eliza hoped she would be forgiven), Walter had insisted he could smell snow and that it would be with them by tomorrow morning. Eliza wasn't entirely convinced that he wasn't pulling her leg; she had no idea what snow was supposed to smell like, or that it had any kind of smell at all.

She might get to find out in the morning, and she was strangely excited at the prospect: Aukland didn't get much in the way of snow, although there had been a blizzard several years ago which she only vaguely remembered.

A glance at her phone informed her that it was time to leave and she hurried downstairs, hooking her coat off the peg by the front door and hastily donning it. She was being picked up by Jay again, but this time she wouldn't be on her own with him for the short drive into the village. Maisie was travelling with them, whilst Dulcie, Beth and Walter were hitching a lift with Otto. Petra and her husband would also be joining them, as would Amos and his partner, Lena. It was going to be quite a crowd, and Eliza was apprehensive. Although she'd met most of them before, she wasn't used to so many people at once, and they were still relative strangers – even the two that **were** actual relatives!

Eliza hurried towards the car, got in and buckled up, saying hello as she did so, then blushing when she caught Jay's eye as he glanced in the rear-view mirror. 'Thank you for inviting me to Christmas lunch,' she said. 'It's very kind of you.'

'Blame Walter,' he replied with a smile. 'He insisted that you be subjected to the

Fairfax version of festive fun. I think he wants a buffer between him and us, and I'm sorry to say that you're it. You'll probably wish you'd stayed at the cottage by the end of it. We can be a rowdy bunch.'

Maisie huffed. 'Speak for yourself.' She swivelled around to look over her shoulder at Eliza. 'I'm the quiet one.'

'Only because you've got your head in the clouds most of the time. Maisie is a daydreamer.' he added, speaking to Eliza. 'Or maybe a butterfly, flitting from one thing to the next. You've yet to find your niche in life, eh, Maisie?'

Eliza could hear the genuine affection in his voice as he teased his sister.

'Has Nikki been moaning again?' Maisie sounded cross. 'Just because she knew she wanted to be a teacher when she was six... Did you always want to be an artist?' she asked Eliza.

Eliza laughed. 'When I was growing up I wanted to be a hairdresser.'

'What made you change your mind?'

'My dad: he encouraged me to draw and paint, and the day I sold my very first painting I decided I wanted to be an artist instead.'

'How old were you?'

'Fifteen.'

'Gosh, I'm twenty-five, and I still don't know what I want to be when I grow up!' Maisie exclaimed.

'Sis, you **are** grown up,' Jay laughed.

She moaned, 'So why does everyone still treat me like a kid?'

'Because you're the baby of the family?'

'I thought that was supposed to be Sammy,' Maisie retorted. She smirked at him. 'Do me a favour and give Mum another grandchild, so the heat's off me.'

'Hey, ask Dulcie! She's the one with a partner.'

'I did. She said she can't think about having children just yet.'

'But I **can**?' Jay sounded amused.

Eliza thought it quite informative; in just a couple of minutes she had learnt that Jay was single and childless. Not that it mattered, of course...

Her train of thought was derailed as The Black Horse, the pub she had noticed on Monday night from the backseat of the taxi, came into view, and her chest constricted when she thought of all the people who would be there, some of whom she had only just met and others who would be total strangers.

She needn't have worried, though. She was made to feel very welcome, even if most of the chat went over her head, and she was content to listen to the various conversations flowing around her, answering the occasional question that was asked of her, and generally trying to take it all in.

Amos's partner, Lena (a cheerful woman in her sixties), was in the middle of telling them about something she called 'the wedding of the year,' which involved a woman by the name of October and a guy who owned a horse and could afford a big swanky do, when a blare of noise interrupted her.

It was coming from the corner of the room where a microphone had been set up, and Eliza's heart sank as she glanced up at the TV screen on the wall above it. It had burst into life with colourful flashing images and the words 'Sing Your Heart Out'. Yippee, karaoke, her favourite – **not** – and she shuddered at the thought of hearing yet another rendition of **Riptide** by Vance Joy.

'Is that what I think it is?' Jay asked Dulcie, nodding towards the setup in the corner.

Dulcie beamed. 'It is.'

'Why didn't you tell me it was karaoke night?' he groaned.

'Because you wouldn't have come?'

'Damn right, I wouldn't have.' He caught Eliza's eye, and she bit her lip. He looked as dismayed as she felt, and for some reason, she was pleased to discover that they had a dislike of karaoke in common.

'The Black Horse doesn't usually do karaoke,' his sister was saying. 'This is an exception. We get to sing along to Christmas songs, so think of it as a kind of carol service, but with wine and better music.'

Jay rolled his eyes and Eliza giggled. Maybe this wouldn't be so bad, she mused. She rather enjoyed a carol service.

With only three days to go until Christmas Day, the pub was very festive, and she particularly liked the log burner that pumped out lovely warmth from its home in the chimney breast. She had yet to find the courage to light the one in the cottage after it had gone out sometime during the early hours of Tuesday morning, but perhaps she would give it a go tomorrow. She planned on having a lie-in, doing some sketching and perhaps reading one of the books on the shelves in the cottage's living room. After two days of travelling followed by two days of meeting her uncle and his new family and being engulfed in their hectic lives, Eliza could do with a quiet day to recharge her batteries and give herself time to reflect.

But right this instant there was no chance of being quiet because the karaoke machine had kicked into life with the lively tune by Wizzard, and the whole pub began to sing along to the lyrics of **I Wish It Could Be Christmas Every Day** – with the exception of herself and Jay, who looked thunderstruck at the eruption of noise. Then he saw her gazing at him, gave a reluctant smile and a shrug, and began to sing.

Not wanting to feel left out, Eliza tried a tentative warble, aware that her singing voice left a lot to be desired, but she was soon belting out the tune as enthusiastically as the rest of them.

Several songs later, there was a brief respite for drinks to be refreshed, then it was all go again as **Merry Christmas Everyone** filled the air.

By the time the sing-along was over, Eliza was hoarse but happy. She hadn't had this much fun in ages, and she was incredibly grateful to Dulcie for inviting her this evening. The alternative – watching unfamiliar TV, in an unfamiliar house, all by herself – hadn't been a particularly appealing prospect.

It took ages for everyone to say goodnight, with lots of to-ing and fro-ing, and hugs and kisses on cheeks, but eventually Eliza found herself in the back seat of Jay's car once again and bouncing slowly up Muddypuddle Lane.

Jay insisted on driving as far as the little parking area reserved for the residents of Petra's cottages instead of dropping her in the lane, and when Eliza clambered out of the vehicle, she found that he had already got out.

'I'll walk you to your door,' he said, holding his phone aloft, the beam from it illuminating the path.

'You needn't bother, I'll be fine,' she replied not wanting to put him out. No doubt he would be glad to get back to the farmhouse after such a raucous evening.

'Humour me,' he said, falling into step alongside her. He cleared his throat and she sensed he felt awkward. 'I don't know about you, but my ears are ringing.'

'Mine, too,' she giggled. 'It was fun though.'

'Yeah, it was. Er, what are you doing tomorrow?'

'I thought I'd have a quiet day, pottering around the cottage.' She came to a stop outside the front door, the glow of the lamp that she'd left on before she went out visible through the living room curtains. It was enough to illuminate Jay's face.

'In that case, would you like to come to a nativity play? Petra is holding one at the stables, and Dulcie has ordered everyone to come along to show their support.' He huffed. 'If I've got to go, I don't see why **you** shouldn't have to, considering you're one of the family now.'

One of the family... was that how Jay viewed her? The thought was as lovely as it was disappointing – for reasons she would attempt to analyse later.

'How can I resist such a charming invitation?' she teased. 'What time?'

'Three o'clock. I'll see you there. Oh, and dress warmly. It's held in the arena but apparently it's colder inside, than out. Or so Dulcie reckons. Frankly, I'd be surprised if she has ever been in it: she doesn't like horses much.'

'I do,' Eliza said. 'I used to ride when I was younger.'

'Rounding up sheep on horseback?' Jay teased.

Eliza rolled her eyes. 'Why does everyone think of sheep when they think of New Zealand?' she shot back. 'We have plenty of other animals; but they're not too keen on being herded, though.'

'Such as?'

'How about seals?'

'Now you're talking.'

'Platypuses and echidnas?' she continued.

Jay groaned, 'Stop talking dirty to me.' Then he looked horrified and winced. 'Sorry, I didn't mean that the way it sounded.'

Eliza tried unsuccessfully to stifle a giggle. 'I take it you're fond of wildlife?'

'It kinda goes with the territory,' he said. 'I don't just install listening equipment, I help analyse the results, too. I might never see the creatures who make most of the noises I hear, but when I do... oh, man. It's such a privilege.'

Eliza felt the same. 'You'll have to come visit me sometime,' she said lightly. 'I might be biased, but Ruakaka is one of the best places for wildlife.'

'I might take you up on that.' He was looking into her eyes, his expression unreadable, and Eliza had a sudden vision of him in the hammock outside her bach, a hat over his face and a tinny in his hand. In her mind's eye, he looked as though he belonged there.

The vision dissolved when Maisie called from the car, 'Jay? What are you doing?'

'I'll be there in a sec,' he shouted back, his eyes not leaving Eliza's. 'See you tomorrow?'

She nodded, not trusting herself to speak. The image had sent a shiver down the back of her neck, and desire stirred in her stomach.

His voice was soft as he said, 'Sleep tight, Eliza.' And with that, he turned on his heel and headed off up the path.

She watched until he was out of sight. Watching him as he walked away was becoming a habit.

Eliza's head was bent over the drawing pad, her pencil moving in quick, decisive strokes. Every so often she would refer to the photo on her phone to ensure the angle was right, but the true essence of the delight on Maisie's face was only coming to life in the sketch she was drawing.

The living room light overhead wasn't the best, but it was bright enough to sketch by, so when Eliza had found herself strangely restless (she should have been bushed after the busy, exciting day she'd had) she'd resorted to doing the one thing guaranteed to soothe and calm her – she drew.

As well as the sketch she was currently working on, several more drawings lay scattered across the table. She had been working for a couple of hours, unable to stop until she'd got the urge to create out of her system (for the time being) but she vowed to call it a day when she finished this one. It was late – or early, depending on one's perspective – and she should try to get some sleep, else she would be fit for nothing tomorrow.

Happy with what she'd done so far, she put her pencil down and surveyed the pieces of work critically. Maisie, face-to-face with the cutest of the pygmy goats; Sammy with his pup, Tara, licking his face; and a pastiche of all four of the Fairfax siblings, which still needed a great deal of work.

She also had the beginnings of a drawing of the farmhouse and yard (similar to the one hanging in Walter's house) and a very brief sketch of what she remembered of Otto's new restaurant.

She would paint the ones she could in the morning, when the kitchen was flooded with natural daylight, and resume work on the others later. But for now, she was done.

There was one painting that she wanted to do that she had yet to begin work on though, but that would have to wait until another time.

Exhaustion overwhelmed her, and she dropped her head into her hands and tried to find the energy to take herself off to bed.

But as she sat there sleepily, she became aware of the absolute silence filling the cottage.

It was unnerving and rather eerie.

Eliza straightened up, her eyes darting around the room. There wasn't so much as the tick of a clock to break the silence, and she was acutely aware of how isolated and alone she was in this little cottage. Her neighbours had left and the nearest people were up at the farm.

There was no one she could call on for help, should anything happen.

She got to her feet, feeling silly, and told herself off. **Of course** there were people she could call on: there was Petra for one, and there was always Walter or Jay.

Jay...

Her thoughts had kept circling back to him whilst she was working tonight, and she guessed he might have played some part in her restlessness.

Gah, she needed to get some sleep, but this blanketing silence was disconcerting. She could have sworn it hadn't been this quiet last night, or the night before.

Telling herself she was being a wimp, and trying to ignore the fact that it didn't matter how many numbers she had in her phone as there was no signal anyway, she got to her feet. It was time for bed. A good night's rest was all that was needed to put such fanciful thoughts out of her head.

But when she switched off the living room light, there was a strange glow coming from outside. The room should have been in darkness, but she could see far better than she should have been able to, and she eased the curtain aside, wondering if Petra had left an outside light on.

Eliza gasped at the sight before her.

Snow!

It was falling thickly in big fat flakes, and there was already a covering on the ground and a little layer had even accumulated on the windowsill.

Mesmerised, Eliza watched the snow drift lazily out of the sky, and her heart swelled at the beauty of the scene in front of her.

At that moment, Eliza felt happier than she had felt in a very long time.

CHAPTER FIVE

'It's been snowing,' Maisie announced, as Jay bounded into the kitchen, bright-eyed and bushy-tailed, eager to go outside and play. He had planned to work on Sammy's present some more today, but how could he resist that lovely snow!

'So I see. Great, isn't it!' he cried, snatching a slice of toast off her plate and cramming it into his mouth before she could object. Sometimes, he could be as childish as his youngest sister, and the sight of the snow-covered valley when he'd opened the curtains seemed to have brought out the big kid in him.

It had been years since he'd seen snow!

'Do you think the goats will be warm enough?' Maisie asked, worriedly.

'They're in the barn with lots of hay and straw, and they've got fur coats to keep them warm,' he told her.

'Dulcie said the same thing.'

'There you go, then!'

'But Dulcie doesn't know any more than I do about keeping goats.'

'Petra does, so Dulcie can always ask her. Wanna come outside?'

'I've been outside. It's cold.'

'You're no fun.'

Maisie sent him an arched look. 'Why don't you ask Eliza? You seem really into her.'

Jay was about to retort, when he hesitated. Was it so obvious that he fancied her? But fancying someone and doing something about it was a completely different box of frogs. He might be attracted to her and he might enjoy her company, but that didn't mean he was going to proposition her, not with her being part of Walter's family, and therefore part of his by Dulcie's association with Otto. Imagine if he did and she rebuffed him? It would make the rest of her stay here awkward for both of them.

But what if she didn't? What if she was as attracted to him as he was to her? Would it be awkward then?

Maybe... Especially when it was time for them to go their separate ways.

Then again, he had been in the same situation before, several times, and it had turned out alright, with both parties knowing full well that the relationship would only last a short while.

Which was why he was never going to settle down, he said to himself. Or, not for some considerable time at least. It simply wasn't feasible unless the woman in question was happy to follow him around the world.

Putting those thoughts to one side and ignoring the fact that he no longer had a job that took him around the world (unless he landed another contract) he made a mug of coffee and went to see if there was a pair of wellies he could borrow, and some gloves. He could feel a snowman-making session coming on!

Despite having had only five hours sleep, as soon as Eliza opened her eyes she was instantly alert, as the memory of sitting at the window in the middle of the night and watching the snow fall from a leaden sky popped into her head.

Pushing the covers back, she leapt out of bed and raced to the window, and when she opened the curtains the sight had her gasping and laughing in equal measures.

The world was white, a stark contrast to the clear pale blue sky and watery sun, and she couldn't wait to go outside.

Ignoring her rumbling tummy, she threw on some clothes and scampered downstairs, lamenting her lack of waterproof boots as she dragged on her coat and opened the door.

To her amazement, it wasn't as cold as she'd assumed (although it was far chillier than she was used to) so she decided to walk up to the stables to ask whether the planned nativity play was still going ahead. She also wanted to take a photo or two of the farm, in order for her to complete her drawing this evening, so she set off gingerly, hoping the snow wasn't be as slippery as it looked.

It wasn't, and neither was it particularly deep – a few centimetres at most – but it crunched underfoot in a very satisfactory way and she had great pleasure in stamping along the path and leaving her footprints in the virgin snow. She even drew a heart in the snow-covered banking, standing back to admire her handiwork and smiling broadly.

The low rumble of an engine interrupted her fun, and she glanced in the direction of the lane. A tractor was moving slowly up it, and she wondered whether it was clearing the road.

Resuming her trek up the path to the stables, Eliza found several equine heads poking over the top of their stalls, ears flicking back and forth.

A woman was walking across the yard pushing a wheelbarrow with a fork poking out of the pungent pile it contained, and she halted when she spied Eliza. 'Can I help you?'

'Hi, I'm looking for Petra? I'm staying in one of the cottages down the way.'

'You must be Eliza. I've heard all about you. I'm Charity. I help out now and again. I think she's up at the house.'

'Thanks.' Eliza stopped to stroke a nose or two, breathing in the comforting smell of horse and wondering whether she would be able to book a hack. She had always wanted to ride in the snow and today would be perfect. However, she guessed Petra probably had her hands full with the nativity play (assuming it was still going ahead) so maybe she could book it another time. It would be good to get on the back of a horse again.

She knocked at the door and when Petra yelled, 'Come in,' Eliza tentatively stepped inside. Mindful of her snow-covered boots, she slipped them off and waggled her cold damp toes. Those boots weren't meant to be worn in the snow, or the rain for that matter.

'Take your socks off and put them on the radiator,' Petra instructed, coming into the hall and seeing her predicament. Her son appeared behind her, toddling determinedly towards the door, and she scooped him up, ignoring his protests. She said, with a grin. 'Amory has just learnt to walk, and now there's no stopping him.'

Petra's pride was obvious, and after Eliza had removed her wet socks and draped them on the radiator, she chucked the child under the chin. The little boy's lip quivered, and he gazed at her petulantly.

'I don't think he's very impressed with me,' Eliza said.

'He's not impressed with me right now either, so don't take it personally,' his mother said. 'Come through; there's a pot of coffee on the go and a slice of cake, if you fancy it.'

Eliza's tummy rumbled, and she laughed. 'I'd love some, please. I didn't bother with breakfast.'

'In that case, I can furnish you with a sausage sandwich, if you like?'

Eliza was sorely tempted. 'No thanks, cake will be fine.'

'It's no bother,' Petra insisted, leading her into a large kitchen where her husband, Harry, was seated at the scrubbed pine table, along with two other people. She continued, 'Nellie and Isaac have already had one, so I've got a couple of sausages going spare. If you don't eat them, they'll end up in the dogs.'

The dogs in question, the black spaniel who Eliza had seen before, and a brown and white terrier with a patch over one eye, stared at her balefully, as though daring her to deprive them of their breakfast.

'In that case, I'd love one,' she said, sending a silent 'sorry' to the dogs.

Petra handed Amory to his father and busied herself making the sausage sandwich, talking as she did so. 'This is Nelly and Isaac. Isaac is the architect who drew up the plans for the cottage you are staying in, and Nelly owns the building firm that did the construction. They're here this morning because Harry, bless him, thinks we need to build a hostel and offer riding holidays – as if I haven't got enough on my plate already.' She jabbed a knife in Eliza's direction and said to the couple, 'This is Eliza – she's staying in the middle cottage.'

Harry grinned. 'My idea of turning the cow shed into holiday lets was a good one, wasn't it?'

'Everyone is allowed one good idea in their life,' Petra retorted, but she was smiling to show she didn't mean it.

'How do you like the cottage?' Isaac asked.

'It's lovely,' Eliza said.

Nelly laughed, 'Stop fishing for complements.'

Isaac looked affronted. 'I just wanted some feedback,' he protested.

'You had feedback from your mum and dad. They were your guinea pigs when they stayed in one.'

Petra placed the sandwich on the table in front of Eliza, who uttered her thanks then picked it up and bit into it with enthusiasm.

'How **are** Julia and Stephen?' Petra asked Isaac as she reached for the coffee pot.

Julia? Eliza's ears pricked up. Was that a coincidence, she wondered, as she chewed.

Petra was saying, 'I haven't seen them for ages – not since the wedding. Ask them if they'd like to come to the nativity play this afternoon. As you saw, Nathan has cleared and salted the lane and the car park, and I believe the main roads are clear.'

'They are,' Nelly confirmed. 'The gritters were out last night.'

'I'll ask,' Isaac said. 'They did go to the summer fete, but you must have missed them.'

'I spent most of the day organising the gymkhana,' Petra explained. She turned to Eliza. 'Sorry, this must be boring for you, prattling on about people you don't know. Julia and Stephen are Isaac's parents, and they were the very first guests to stay in the cottages.'

'How long are you here for?' Nelly asked.

'Until the second of January.'

'Is that an Australian accent, I hear?' The woman tilted her head to the side.

'Not quite,' Eliza replied, and Petra leapt in with, 'Sorry, I should have mentioned when I introduced you, that Eliza is Walter's niece, over from New Zealand.'

Isaac was frowning. 'Walter's niece? As in, **Emrys's** daughter? Goodness me!'

And suddenly Eliza knew without a shadow of a doubt that this man's mother was the same woman who her father had been in love with all those years ago.

Eliza tried to concentrate on the nativity play, but she couldn't. She had arrived early and had been scooped up by Dulcie and the rest of the family, who insisted that she joined them, and she was now seated between Walter, on her right, and Jay, on her left. But instead of enjoying the experience, she was craning her neck to look for Isaac, and wondering if any of the women in the arena's viewing gallery might be Julia.

Eliza managed to laugh in all the right places, clap when everyone else did, and look suitably enchanted at the 'ahhh' moments as the youngsters recited their lines. But neither her attention nor her heart had been truly in it, and as the play drew to an end, she felt guilty for not being as invested as she should, seeing how kind Petra had been earlier. The woman had obviously put a great deal of effort into it, and it had been wasted on her.

However, Eliza couldn't help how she felt, or how distracted she was, so when she found an opportunity to speak to Petra, she took it.

'Great play. The children were wonderful,' she said, taking a hot chocolate from a tray that one of the youngsters was holding. Several children were circulating with drinks and nibbles, and the old people from the care home in Picklewick were tucking in with enthusiasm.

Petra saw the direction of her gaze. 'I do it for them, mainly,' she said. 'I did worry that William, the care home's manager, might cry off because of the roads, but he decided it was safe enough, and they look forward to it so much.'

'They seem to be having a great time,' Eliza agreed. 'Did your other guests manage to make it?'

'Which ones?'

'Um, Julia and... Stephen?' Eliza struggled to remember the man's name but the woman's was seared on her mind.

'Yes, they did.'

'I know this sounds odd, but do you mind pointing Julia out to me?'

'May I know why?'

'My dad used to know her.'

'Emrys did?' Petra pursed her lips, and understanding flared in her eyes. 'I see. I suppose it's okay. But before I do, can you promise me that you'll speak to her privately and not in front of her husband.'

'Oh?'

'Last year, her marriage went through a difficult patch. I don't know the full details and neither do I want to, but I believe it was triggered by a certain phone call from New Zealand.' Petra gave her a knowing look.

Eliza's eyes widened and her mouth fell open. She closed it slowly and took a deep breath. It was clearly **her** phone call to Julia to which Petra was referring.

Petra added, 'I'll ask her to pop along to my office. You can chat there. It's the second door on the left as you leave the gallery.'

'Thank you.'

'I'm not saying she'll want to speak to you, mind,' Petra warned, 'but if she does, I'd appreciate it if you didn't upset her.'

'I'll try not to,' Eliza replied, wondering whether she was doing the right thing. Might it be prudent to let sleeping dogs lie?

She hurried along to the office and slipped inside, closing the door behind her. Briefly, she debated whether to pop back to the arena and tell Walter, or someone, where she was, in case they were looking for her, but as she dithered there was a knock on the door.

Eliza watched the handle move as the door slowly opened, and her eyes shot to the woman coming into view.

Julia looked puzzled and a little cross. 'Petra said someone wanted to see me, but she refused to tell me who or why.' Eliza could hear irritation in the woman's voice. 'I must say, I'm not too keen on all this cloak and dagger stuff.'

'Sorry.' Eliza was immediately on the back foot. 'It's me: I wanted to see you.' Her Kiwi twang was more noticeable next to the woman's clipped English tones.

Julia narrowed her eyes. 'Why? Who are you?' But there was a hint of wariness in her face, as though she had already guessed.

Eliza drew in a deep breath. 'I'm Emrys's daughter. We spoke on the phone.'

The woman froze. She looked alarmed and Eliza stepped forward. Julia took a corresponding step back, then glanced over her shoulder. People were leaving the viewing gallery and the corridor outside the office was noisy.

Eliza said hurriedly, 'Please, let me explain.'

'Sorry, I have to go. My husband will be wondering where I am.'

'I'm not here to cause trouble.'

'Trouble?' Julia's voice was sharp.

'Petra suggested there might have been a few issues between you and your husband after I spoke to you. I'm sorry if I was the cause.'

Her face softening, Julia said, 'It wasn't your fault. Thank you for informing me of your father's death.'

'Did you love him?' Eliza blurted.

Julia hesitated, then seemed to come to a decision. 'I can't talk here, but if you want to meet for a coffee after Christmas...?'

Eliza sighed with relief. 'I fly back to New Zealand on the second of January, so it'll have to be before then.'

She didn't know why it was so imperative that she found out more about her father's and Julia's relationship – it just **was.**

Julia said, 'There's a cafe called Rossi near the town hall in Thornbury. Shall we say next Thursday at ten o'clock?'

'I'll be there,' Eliza promised.

Julia nodded once and turned to the door. But before she stepped through it, she said softly, 'I can see him in you.'

Then she was gone, leaving Eliza with tears trickling down her face.

'There you are!' Jay had been sent to look for Eliza by Walter, who wanted to ask her to have tea with him this evening but was worried that she had already left.

Jay had been on his way to the cottage, hoping to catch up with her, but just as he was about to leave the gallery a woman stepped out of a room, hurrying past, and when he glanced inside he spied Eliza.

It appeared to be an office, with a desk strewn with papers and a large whiteboard covered in marker pen on one wall. On another was shelf after shelf of riding hats.

Eliza stood in the middle of the room, her shoulders hunched. Her head was bowed and she was half-turned away from the open door.

'Walter sent me to—' Jay began but broke off abruptly. Unless he was very much mistaken, Eliza was crying. She was brushing at her cheeks with her fingers and her shoulders were shaking. 'What's wrong?' Instinctively he glanced behind him but there was no sign of the woman. 'Did that woman upset you?'

'Yes. No.' Eliza's voice wobbled. 'It's not her fault.'

'Can I do anything?'

'Not really.'

'Do you want to talk about it?'

She bit her lip and stared at the floor, and he assumed she didn't, but then she nodded and said, 'Not here – at the cottage?'

'I'll just go tell Walter. He sent me to find you because he wants to know if you'll have tea with him this evening. Just you and him.'

'I'd like that.'

'He also told me to tell you he does a mean hotpot.'

That raised a smile, albeit a small one, and Jay was relieved.

'What time does he want me?' she asked.

'Six?'

'Tell him I'll be there.'

'I'll see you back at the cottage,' he said, and hurried to deliver the message to Walter.

There was no sign of the woman he had seen coming out of the office a few moments ago, and Jay wondered what she could have said or done to make Eliza cry.

After telling Walter that Eliza would love to have tea with him, Jay found Petra and thanked her, congratulating her on a successful nativity play, then he squeezed past the numerous old folks who appeared reluctant to leave, and jogged across the yard and down the path leading to the row of holiday cottages.

The door to the one Eliza was staying in was ajar, so he knocked and went inside, looking around curiously.

He had stepped straight into the sitting room, and although it was small, it had a nice squashy couch, an armchair and a telly at one end. At the other was a dining table situated in front of patio doors which led out to a small courtyard-type garden.

The room was warm, cosy, and festive, and he could tell that Petra had made an effort to make her guest feel welcome over the Christmas period.

On hearing noises coming from the kitchen, he called, 'Hello?' not wanting to startle Eliza.

'I'm making a pot of tea,' she called back. 'Would you like a cup?'

'Please.' He moved closer until she came into view, and studied her carefully as she made the tea. She looked perkier than she had a few minutes ago, he was relieved to find, and she even managed another smile when she saw him looming in the doorway.

'The cottage is nice,' he said, hunting around for something to say.

'It's lovely,' she agreed. 'Milk and sugar?'

'Just milk.' He watched her pour the tea into two mugs, from a proper teapot, then add a drop of milk.

She gave them a quick stir, then handed one to him.

'Shall we go sit down?' she suggested, and he stepped back into the living room, taking a seat on the sofa.

'I bet it's toasty in here when that's lit,' he observed, after an awkward silence where neither of them seemed to know what to say. He jerked his chin at the small log burner.

'It would be if I knew how to get it going.'

'Would you like me to show you?' Over the years, Jay had lit a fair few fires in his time. Crouching down on the floor, he opened the front of it, aware that Eliza had joined him on the rug.

She was watching intently as he scrunched up a couple of sheets of the newspapers that had been placed neatly in a basket next to the burner, along with kindling and some suitably sized logs.

She was so close that her knee was touching his thigh, and he could smell her perfume – a light, floral scent that reminded him of summer meadows. His heart skipped a beat when she leant even closer to study the way he was stacking the kindling on top of the newspaper.

'You need something that catches light quickly,' he explained. 'That's what the newspaper is for. And something that burns easily but a little slower, like these sticks. Then the logs go on one at a time, but only when the kindling has caught. If you put too many on at once, you run the risk of smothering the fire before it has a chance to get going.' He reached for the box of matches on the mantlepiece and struck one, holding the flame against the scrunched-up newspaper until it caught.

Slowly the fire ate through the paper, and he thought it had gone out, but with a little spark a piece of kindling caught, and pretty soon he had a small blaze going.

After adding some logs and watching it for a while, Jay was confident that the fire wouldn't go out. He sat back on his heels.

Eliza was gazing into the flames, a distant look on her face. Her skin glowed, and the fire flickered in her eyes. 'I guess you're wondering what all that was about?' she said.

'You don't have to tell me, if you don't want to.'

She didn't seem to have heard. 'She said she can see my dad in me.'

Jay was confused. 'Is that a bad thing?'

'No, it's a good thing.' She glanced up at him. 'No one's ever said that before. I look nothing like him, you see; I take after my mother.'

There was silence for a moment, then Jay said softly, 'Maybe she wasn't referring to your looks?'

Another silence.

Jay risked a glance in her direction and was dismayed to see Eliza crying again. Tears were trickling quietly down her face, and her expression was so sad that his heart went out to her.

Without thinking, he scooted closer and put his arm around her, pulling her into him. Resting his cheek lightly on the top of her head, he gently rubbed her arm and waited.

'I'm sorry,' she sniffed after a few minutes. 'What must you think of me?'

'Do you feel able to talk about it? Do I need to thump someone?'

She uttered a croaky laugh. 'No, no thumping needed.'

Jay felt quite bereft when she sat up to brush away the tears with her fingers, and he told himself to stop being a jerk. To his shame, he had enjoyed holding her far too much, given the circumstances.

'My dad – Walter's brother – died two years ago, and nothing's felt right since,' she began, drawing her knees into her chest and wrapping her arms around her legs as she stared into the fire. Jay put another log on it and closed the burner's door.

'He was my champion, you know?' she continued. 'He always had my back and fought my corner. When Mum tried to get me to study **something sensible**—' Eliza did air quotes '—Dad told her to let me be, that I had to tread my own path.'

'As an artist?'

She nodded. 'Mum wanted me to have a **proper job**, get married and settle down, like my sister, Cathy.' Her laugh had a bitter edge. 'I failed on both counts. My job is precarious, I live in what she calls a shack, and my marriage fell apart after a couple of years. I think I'm a big disappointment to her.'

Jay didn't know what to say to that, so he said nothing.

Eventually she carried on. 'I miss my dad so much, and I just wanted to see where he was born, where he spent the first part of his life. I suggested that we all go to the UK, as a kind of homage to him, but Mum was dead against it and Cathy wasn't interested. Mum claimed she couldn't face all the travelling, and she also said she didn't want to rake up the past. She's not happy that I'm here – and I think Julia might be the reason.'

'Julia?'

'After Dad died, I found a note in his papers, asking for a woman by the name of Julia Richards to be contacted in the event of his death.' Eliza turned her gaze on him. 'I believe they had a relationship.'

'They were lovers?'

'Walter seemed to think so.' She shrugged. 'There was definitely something between them.' After a deep sigh, she said, 'I suspect my mum's reluctance to accompany me on this trip might have more to do with Julia, rather than the travelling. Maybe Mum was right: digging up the past wasn't a good idea. Perhaps I shouldn't have come.'

'Did you come here just to find out more about your father and Julia?'

'No, I came here because I wanted to know about Dad's life before he came to New Zealand.'

'And have you?'

'A bit. Walter and I had a long chat.'

'Are you glad you met Walter? And Otto?'

'Yes.' Her reply was emphatic.

'Then you didn't make the wrong decision,' he assured her.

She gave him a rueful smile. 'I've discovered I have a whole new family.'

'Yeah, about that... You may wish you hadn't. My sisters can be very full-on. Not to mention my mum.'

'They're lovely, Dulcie especially.'

'What about me?' he joked. 'Aren't I lovely too?' He was trying to cheer her up and lighten the mood, but when he saw the solemn expression on her face as she gazed soulfully into his eyes, he realised it had backfired. Now was not the time to be making jokes, however well-intentioned.

She continued to stare at him, and he felt the tension in the air. It sizzled between them, an electric current that he was unable to name

Her eyes were large and luminous, glistening from her recent tears, and her face seemed to be growing closer. It was only when her lips parted and she lifted her chin, that he realised he was about to kiss her.

Or she, him...

Without knowing who moved first, his mouth was on hers and a jolt shot through him. Then he was kissing her deeply, his tongue delving between her lips. She entwined her arms around his neck and he sank his fingers into her hair, his other hand resting on the rug behind her as he gently lowered her down, his body covering hers.

Her soft curves lay underneath him, and all he could think of were the sensations coursing through him as the kiss carried him away.

Just as his hand slipped underneath her fleece, a loud crack from a log splitting on the fire brought him to his senses, and he froze.

What was he **doing?**

This was such a bad idea on so many levels. Not only was she a guest of his sister's (in a way), but she was also upset, and he felt as though he was taking advantage of her. Although he badly wanted to make love to her, it went against the grain to do so like this.

Reluctantly, he kissed her softly, the passion dial turned way down, then he released her and sat up.

Eliza lay sprawled on the rug, her lips rosy from his kiss and her pupils so large and deep he feared he might fall headlong into them. Her chest heaved, and when she caught her bottom lip between her teeth and blinked slowly, it took all the control he had not to throw caution to the wind.

'I'd better go,' he said. 'You'll be needing to set off to Walter's soon.' He watched her closely as her eyes regained their focus and the desire drained out of them.

'What? Er... yeah. Walter.' She sat up, adjusting her fleece, and smiled nervously. 'Thanks for listening.' Spots of colour had appeared on her cheeks, and he wondered whether they resulted from embarrassment or arousal.

'It was my pleasure,' he replied warmly.

'Mine, too.' Her voice was low, and her blush deepened.

'I didn't mean...' he began, realising how that sounded, then he trailed off.

With a wry twist of her lips, she said, 'I did.' And without waiting for a response, she scrambled to her feet.

Jay also stood up. 'Will we see you tomorrow?' He said it lightly, saying 'we' instead of 'I' because he didn't want to put any pressure on her, despite hoping she would say yes. There was something about this woman that had captured his imagination. She had fired a spark inside him that burnt brighter each time he saw her.

It did concern him that she had such an effect on him, but he didn't want to think about that now. He simply wanted to see her again – soon.

'Possibly.' Her reply was non-committal. 'I've got some shopping to do.'

'Would you like a lift into the village?'

'I think I'll have to go to Thornbury.'

'I can take you if you like?'

'Are you sure?'

'I'm sure. Ten o'clock?'

When she agreed, some of his tension eased. He told himself that he didn't like the idea of her traipsing around a strange place alone, despite realising she had travelled halfway around the world on her own and was quite capable of taking the bus to a town that was only nine miles away.

But the real reason was that since the first moment he saw her, he hadn't been able to get her out of his mind. And now that he'd kissed her, he had the disturbing feeling he wouldn't be able to get her out of his heart.

CHAPTER SIX

When Eliza woke, the first thought to enter her head was that she had kissed Jay. The second was that it was Christmas Eve and she was nearly twenty thousand kilometres from home.

It was strange to think of her mum doing some last-minute shopping in the summer sunshine to the sound of Christmas tunes in the shops and festive lights in store windows. She could imagine her strolling along Queen Street and eyeing Smith & Caughey's famous Christmas windows. The department store always had the best animated decorations, which usually included handmade puppets and light displays. Her mum would have already picked up the lamb for Christmas lunch, but she would want to buy the veggies and salad stuff fresh, as well as the seafood for the starter and the fruit for the customary pavlova.

Traditionally, Eliza had always made the trip to Aukland to spend the festive season with her parents, although the previous two Christmases had been awful without her dad.

Thinking of her father brought yesterday into sharp relief again, but rather than her mind being filled with Dad and the chat she'd had with Julia, her thoughts centred on Jay.

For a while, she'd thought that he had been about to make love to her, and never had her body craved another's touch as it had craved his. But he had pulled back, and her disappointment had been acute.

All through the delicious meal of lamb hotpot that Walter had made with his own hands (no Otto, this time) Eliza hadn't been able to get Jay out of her mind. Nevertheless, she'd had a lovely evening getting to know Walter better, and he had regaled her with stories of his and her dad's childhood, and had clearly enjoyed reminiscing. Eliza also felt that she had gotten to know her father better too, which was a comfort.

With an hour to go before Jay collected her, Eliza pottered around, getting dressed, eating breakfast, and looking over the work she had done after she'd got back from Walter's yesterday evening. She'd been forced to paint without the benefit of daylight, but she was pleased when she saw the results of her efforts this morning, as the weak winter sun shone through the window illuminating the pictures sitting on the table.

They were nowhere near her best work, but they weren't her worst either, and she decided they would do. All except one. She picked it up and examined it, trying to work out what was lacking, but it eluded her for the moment.

Irritated, she gathered up the others and took them upstairs to lay them on the mattress in the spare bedroom. They were dry, so they would be fine there until she was ready to mount and frame them. **If,** that is, she could find a shop in Thornbury that sold ready-cut mounts and frames.

Luckily, the drawing pad she used was a standard A4 size, so she shouldn't have any difficulty buying frames for the paintings and if she had to do without the cardboard mounts, then so be it.

She'd just finished getting ready when she heard Jay's car pull up. Grabbing her coat and bag, she hurried out to meet him, slipping into the passenger seat with a tentative smile, unsure how to behave after yesterday's kiss.

To her relief, he smiled back, as open and sunny as always, and she began to wonder whether he was going to pretend it had never happened.

She wished she could!

Although she didn't regret it as such (it had been far too exciting for that) she knew it had been reckless. Eliza was self-aware enough to know that she had a tendency to give her heart too freely, and that if she gave her heart to Jay she would get hurt. Not because he was a bad person, but because there was no hope of any kind of relationship beyond the short time she would spend in this country.

It didn't take long to drive to Thornbury, but it took considerably longer to find a free parking space. The town was busy, and the atmosphere was extremely festive; there was a sense of anticipation in the air, and also a sense of urgency as people hurried to and fro to finish their Christmas shopping.

'What exactly is it you need?' Jay asked as they wandered down the high street.

'I'm looking for a shop selling picture frames,' Eliza replied.

'Shall we try down here?' Jay pointed to a side street that seemed to have fewer chain stores and more independent shops.

'We can give it a go,' she said, and was surprised when Jay took hold of her hand. It was busy, and they had to dodge and sidestep elderly people, pushchairs, and groups of teenagers. Anxious not to lose him, Eliza gripped Jay's hand tightly. At least, that's what she tried to tell herself. The real reason was that she found she enjoyed the contact very much indeed.

It took her a while, but she eventually spotted a shop that seemed promising and went inside, and a short while later she emerged clutching several frames of the same size that had mounts already built into them. All she needed now was wrapping paper and greeting cards, and her shopping was done.

'Do you mind if we stop off for a coffee?' Jay asked.

'Not at all.'

'Actually, I was thinking perhaps you could have a coffee while you wait for me?'

'Why? Where are you going?'

'I've got some errands to run. I won't be long, I promise.'

A short way down the street was a cafe and she went inside, bemused, wondering what Jay was up to that he didn't want her to see. The thought briefly crossed her mind that he might want to pop into a chemist for some condoms, and the very idea made her shiver. Perhaps that was why he had stopped kissing her yesterday afternoon? Another shiver travelled down her spine, and she swiftly pushed away the heady thought of Jay making love to her.

Ordering a hot chocolate with decadent cream and fluffy marshmallows on top, she took a seat near the window to keep an eye out for him, and as she sipped her drink she wondered anew why she was taking such a risk. She was in danger of losing her peace of mind if she gave into her base desire to jump his bones.

Eliza almost snorted into her hot chocolate. Jump his bones, indeed! That was hardly romantic, was it? But that was precisely what she felt like doing. She didn't want to take it slow. She wanted to dive headlong into a mad passionate affair, regardless of how soon it might end.

Recognising how reckless those thoughts were, she concentrated on her forthcoming meeting with Julia instead. Thinking about what the woman and her father might have meant to each other certainly served to throw a bucket of cold water on her lust, and by the time Jay eventually returned (which was rather longer than she had anticipated) she was thoroughly in control of herself once more.

Jay strode into the coffee shop, breathless and apologetic. 'Sorry I took so long,' he said, but he didn't offer any further explanation of where he'd been or what he'd done. He wasn't holding any packages or any bags, so she could only assume that whatever it was could be easily concealed in a pocket. Or maybe he'd not been able to find what he wanted? Or maybe his errands hadn't had anything to do with shopping.

Hoping for a clue, she asked, 'Did you get what you wanted?'

Jay blinked. 'Yes, I did, thank you.'

Ah, so he **had** been shopping.

Before she could question him further, he asked, 'Are you done? Is there anywhere else you'd like to go?'

'I just need wrapping paper and Christmas cards,' she said, getting to her feet. He held his hand out for the bag of frames, and she hesitated before passing it to him. 'It's not heavy,' she protested.

'That's not the point. It wouldn't be right, you with your arms full and me not carrying anything. Let's get you that wrapping paper and those cards, then how about we have a quick bite to eat before we head back to Muddypuddle Lane?'

Eliza thought that was a wonderful idea, so the rest of her purchases were made very quickly and they were soon sitting across the table from one another in a small bistro just off Thornbury's main street.

Over a light lunch of hot pulled pork and apple rolls, along with a small glass of white wine for Eliza and a glass of Pepsi for Jay, he advised her that Dulcie expected Eliza to spend the rest of Christmas Eve with the Fairfax family, along with Walter and Otto. The agenda was to walk into Picklewick to attend the carol service at the church and watch the candlelight procession through the village this evening, followed by a late dinner cooked by Otto.

'Poor Otto,' Eliza said, after confirming
that she would be delighted to spend the
evening with them. 'It must be awful for
him to have to do all this cooking and not
be able to join in.'

Jay arched an eyebrow. 'I get the feeling
he enjoys it,' he said with a smile. 'Otto
strikes me as the sort of man who
wouldn't do anything he didn't want to
do. Anyway, from what I understand, he's
going to prepare everything beforehand
so he can come with us to the carol
service.'

'I hope his restaurant is a success,' she
said, taking another bite of her delicious
pork roll.

'So do I. He's invested an awful lot in it,'
Jay said, and went on to explain about
the job offer that had been made to Otto
a couple of months ago by his former

boss in London which he had turned down, finishing with, 'My daft sister is still holding onto vestiges of guilt because she felt Otto has given up an awful lot for her.'

'But anyone can see how happy they are,' Eliza pointed out. The pair of them made her heart melt, they were so much in love. Then there was Nikki and Gio, who, from what Eliza had witnessed, were more reserved, especially around Sammy, but despite that, she could see how devoted they were to each other.

At that moment, she happened to glance away from her plate and up at Jay.

He was staring at her intently, as though he wanted to whisk her off to bed and make love to her until morning.

But what stole her breath and made her heart leap, was the realisation that she would happily let him.

It might be dark and cold this evening, but Jay thought the walk from Muddypuddle Lane to Picklewick across the fields to the church was simply magical.

Snow still lay on the ground, covering the grass in an uneven blanket, and the sky was a clear inky black studded with diamonds. A gibbous moon lit the path to the village, and as he walked alongside Eliza, the snow crunched underfoot and their misty breath hung in the air.

Dulcie and Otto were ahead of them, but Maisie and Beth had opted to take the car into the village with Walter. To his shame, Jay wished that Dulcie and Otto had also driven, so he could have had Eliza all to himself and kissed her under the stars in the snow.

Not a good idea, mate, he admonished silently, as soon as the thought crossed his mind. He had to keep reminding himself of this, because he seemed to be rather forgetful lately. Eliza was dominating his thoughts and was in his mind constantly.

It took about twenty minutes to reach the outskirts of the village where the path leading from the stables met the road into Picklewick, and as they walked along the pavement, Eliza slowed to peer into a garden.

'Aw, isn't that pretty!' she exclaimed. The house it belonged to was draped in twinkling fairy lights and a miniature

Santa's grotto sat in the middle of the lawn. 'Christmas seems so much more Christmassy here than it does in New Zealand.'

'Is that because it's summer there?'

'Probably. I've always wanted to experience a Dickensian Christmas Day, instead of spending it sweltering in the sun with a barbeque on the go.'

'Is that what you'd normally have for Christmas dinner? A barbecue?'

'No, Mum always cooks lamb. That's more traditional in New Zealand, rather than turkey or goose.'

'I don't know anyone who actually has goose. Otto is cooking turkey. He put it in the oven before we left this evening. You ought to see it – it's massive. But I suppose it has to be if it's going to feed ten. My task in the morning is to peel the spuds, Dulcie's is to tackle the carrots – Otto is insisting they are cut into batons and not round slices – and Mum is responsible for the sprouts.'

'Is there anything I can do?'

'Hide,' Jay said dryly.

'What about Maisie? Will she be hiding too?'

Jay pulled a face. 'I don't think Otto trusts her to do anything in the kitchen. Not after she burnt the milk for the hot chocolates the other day. I think she did it on purpose.'

'Surely not!'

He nodded. 'It wouldn't be the first time. Dulcie suggested that Maisie sees to the chickens and the goats, and leave the cooking to everyone else.' He leant in closer, inhaling Eliza's sweet perfume as he added in a whisper, 'I wish I'd thought of that. I'd much prefer to feed goats than peel potatoes.'

'Are you sure I can't help?'

'I'm sure. Relax and enjoy your holiday.'

'It's **your** holiday, too.'

Jay flinched. He still hadn't told anyone that he wouldn't be returning to Borneo. He had decided to leave it until the New Year, in the hope that something would have come up by then, so all he said now was, 'It's my family, therefore I'm obligated to help.'

'I thought you said I was part of it?'

'You are.'

'Well, then. I'll help with the potatoes.'

Jay found he was looking forward to it. Which was strange, because until now he hadn't been too enthused to be given such a chore.

Eliza brought him back to the present when she cried, 'Oh, how lovely!' and pointed to the lychgate. The entrance to the churchyard was festooned in twinkling lights, and the path leading to the porch was lined with flickering candles inside glass lanterns. An organ was playing, and the sweet notes of **Away in a Manger** drifted on the air.

Without warning, it brought a tear to his eye, as the ethereal atmosphere enveloped him in a sense of peace and serenity.

Feeling unusually emotional, Jay's hand sought Eliza's and he wrapped his fingers around it and squeezed lightly. She returned the gesture, her eyes shining, and unable to stop himself, Jay bent his head and kissed her.

She tasted of cinnamon and honey, and her lips were warm and soft. They parted, his tongue slipped between them, seeking hers.

He was so lost in her that he forgot he was standing on the pavement outside a church, until someone pushed past him, muttering, 'Get a room.'

Jay dragged his mouth from Eliza's, his heart hammering, his breathing ragged, and he met her shocked gaze in dismay. 'Sorry,' he stammered, scrambling to turn the heat down on his super-charged emotions. This was neither the time nor the place to give in to such temptation.

'I'm not.' Her reply was soft, but the look in her eyes was anything but. They smouldered and his desire spiked again, slamming into him, making him want to throw her over his shoulder and march back up the hill to her cottage.

'Shall we go inside?' he said instead, his voice gruff.

'I think we'd better, before I suggest something I'll regret,' she replied.

Please suggest it, he almost begged, but held himself in check. Never had he wanted to take a woman to bed more than he wanted to make love with Eliza, and not giving in to his desire was killing him because he sensed she wanted it as much as he.

But this time it wasn't worry about whether it would make things awkward for the rest of their time in Picklewick that held him back; it was because he was worried that he would never want to let her go.

The rest of the Fairfax family, plus Walter, were already inside the church. Jay and Eliza slipped into the pew behind Dulcie and Otto, and for the next forty minutes Jay joined in with the hymn-singing and pretended to listen to the readings. He wasn't a church-going man, but he usually enjoyed the tradition and familiarity of the service, as well as the uplifting and expectant atmosphere. However, on this occasion, all he could concentrate on was Eliza.

The happiness on her face when she collected her Christingle orange, which had cloves inserted into it and a flickering candle on the top, made his heart swell and he couldn't take his eyes off her as she carefully walked down the aisle, shielding the flame with one hand to ensure it didn't go out.

By this point, the lights in the church had been dimmed, and it was lovely to see the procession of candles making their way towards the main door. Once there, people popped them into lanterns stacked on a table and took them outside.

When it was Jay and Eliza's turn, he heard her delighted gasp as she emerged from the church to see a snaking line of bobbing lanterns along the path to the lychgate and beyond, led by Picklewick's vicar.

'I feel like I've stepped back in time,' she said, holding her lantern aloft, her eyes shining. 'I wonder if my dad took part in a ceremony like this when he lived here.'

'He did,' Walter confirmed. 'Every year, until he left home.'

Eliza sighed in satisfaction. 'I was hoping you'd say that. I feel so much closer to him, doing the things he used to do and seeing the things he used to see.'

Jay noticed that the glimmer in her eyes was due to unshed tears, and he put an arm around her shoulder and squeezed gently.

She leant into his side and he inhaled her intoxicating perfume, his heart thudding as she gazed up at him. Never had he wanted to kiss any woman as much as he wanted to kiss Eliza right now, and it was with considerable effort that he pulled his gaze away.

He didn't let go of her, although he did drop his arm, his hand finding hers again, and they proceeded to meander through the village hand-in-hand. And in that moment, one that would be forever etched on his heart, Jay fervently wished that he could hold her hand forever.

Eliza popped a morsel of honey-glazed ham in her mouth and swooned. It was so succulent and flavoursome, that she eagerly ate another mouthful.

'This is divine,' she said to Otto. 'What's your secret?'

He beamed at her. 'Pineapple juice.' Otto gazed around the dinner table, a cheeky grin on his face. 'I've got some left over, if anyone wants a Pina Colada later?'

'Ooh, yes please!' Maisie squealed, and Eliza was sorely tempted.

But when Otto gave her the choice between a Snowball, a blackberry brandy or Baileys Orange Truffle, she was spoilt for choice.

After an impressive meal of cold meats, salad, potatoes and more relishes than she had seen outside of a Pac'N'Save supermarket, Eliza was stuffed. And the salad hadn't just been a few lettuce leaves and tomatoes in a bowl, either! It had been magnificent. The main course was followed by cheese, biscuits and fruit, and Eliza was convinced she couldn't eat another morsel. However, she was certain she could manage a glass of something alcoholic and Christmassy, so she eventually opted for the Snowball, figuring that she might have a taste of the delicious-sounding Baileys later.

With Otto presiding over the drinks in the kitchen (did that man never stop?!) Eliza wandered into the living room.

Seeing the Fairfax family and Walter gathered there, laughing and chatting, sent a sudden blast of homesickness straight through her, and she abruptly realised that it was already Christmas Day in Auckland and had been for several hours.

Jay saw her hovering in the doorway and he beckoned her over. He was sitting on the floor with Sammy (who was beginning to flag) and the pup (who had already flaked out) and he gestured for her to sit next to him.

Eliza hesitated. Ever since Jay had kissed her in the snow outside the church, all she could think about was how much she wanted him, and she wasn't sure how wise it would be to cuddle up on the floor with him. She was already ankle-deep in this man, and she didn't want to sink any deeper because she guessed she might struggle to extricate herself.

Yep, she was a sucker for a handsome face and a fit body; but she had firsthand experience of what handsome could do, and there was no way she was going back to New Zealand with a broken heart simply because she had allowed Jay to have his wicked way with her. She didn't have the type of personality to enjoy a romp between the sheets and for it not to mean anything. She wished she did, because she could give in to her desire, have a thoroughly enjoyable time, and then walk away without a backward glance.

'Are you okay, Eliza?' Dulcie asked. 'You're looking rather pensive.'

'I bet she's missing her mum,' Beth said, sending Eliza a sympathetic look. 'It can't be easy being away from your family at Christmas. Why don't you give her a call? You'll feel better after you talk to her.' Beth glanced at the clock on the dining room wall. 'What time is it in New Zealand?'

'About nine-thirty,' Eliza said. It was a good idea to call her mum, and it would also give her an excuse to have a few minutes away from Jay.

'Go on, what are you waiting for?' Beth urged.

'Privacy?' Walter muttered under his breath.

He might have spoken quietly but Beth heard. 'She can have as much privacy as she wants.' She stuck out her chin and glared at him.

Dulcie got to her feet. 'Come with me. I'll give you the wifi password and you can go upstairs and talk in peace.' She raised her eyebrows at Walter, who nodded his approval.

After telling her the password, Dulcie shoved Eliza towards the stairs. 'Take as long as you need. I'll make sure you won't be disturbed.'

It was kind of Dulcie, but Eliza was already disturbed, and it was Dulcie's brother who was doing the disturbing.

She trotted upstairs, eager to speak to her mum, hoping she would be up by now.

'Where on earth are you?' were her mother's first words when the video call connected.

'Lilac Tree Farm.'

'It looks as though you're in a cave.' Her mum was peering at the screen, her face filling it. She had a dab of sunscreen on the bridge of her nose and Eliza guessed that she, along with Cathy and Toby, Cathy's husband, were out on the deck, enjoying breakfast in the sun.

'I'm at the top of the stairs,' she explained.

'Why are you at the top of the stairs?'

A burst of raucous laughter drifted up from the living room and Eliza smiled. 'That's why. It's noisy down there.'

'You appear to be having a good time,' her mother sniffed.

'I am.' She was having the best time ever, and her homesickness abruptly faded in the face of her mother's obvious disapproval.

Honestly! Her mum could at least be thankful that Eliza wasn't spending Christmas Eve on her own. But then again, it would have given her an opportunity to say 'I told you so,' and crow that Eliza should have stayed in New Zealand and not gone traipsing halfway around the world.

Eliza changed the subject to one more to her mother's liking. 'How's Cathy?'

'The morning sickness has stopped, thank God, and about time too. She's twenty-eight weeks now. Hopefully, she can enjoy her lunch.'

'Is she visiting her in-laws this year?'

Another sniff. 'She and Toby are leaving the day after tomorrow, so I'll be all alone for New Year.'

Great guilt-tripping, Mum, Eliza thought. 'Haven't you been invited to next door's party?'

Her parents used to go to their neighbours' bash every year. Last year Eliza had gone with her. The year before that, Dad's death had been too recent and too raw, and none of them had felt like going anywhere.

'I don't want to go on my own,' her mum complained.

 Eliza held back a sigh. 'You won't **be** on your own. The whole street will be there.' There was more sniffing and when Eliza heard her sister calling in the background, she said with relief, 'I'll let you go,' adding softly, 'Happy Christmas, Mum.'

'Hmm, you too.' A pause followed then, 'Love you, Eliza.'

'Love you, too.' Eliza ended the call with a lump in her throat, and she took a moment to compose herself before joining the others.

When she reached the bottom of the stairs, Jay emerged from the living room and wordlessly took her in his arms. She didn't know how much, if anything, he had heard, but she didn't care if he'd heard every word, because a hug was exactly what she needed.

He held her for several seconds as she clung to him, then he kissed the top of her head, took her by the hand and led her into the bosom of her new, exuberant, and incredibly welcoming family.

CHAPTER SEVEN

Eliza carefully hoisted the bag of presents and stepped outside. It had snowed again overnight (she hadn't been awake to witness it this time) and flakes were still falling, although the cloud layer was lifting.

She thought of Sammy, and the countless other children waking up this Christmas morning to a white world, and she wondered if they felt any of the joy that was coursing through her veins right now. Their parents mightn't be as thrilled, especially if they had places to go and people to see, but Eliza couldn't help feeling thankful that she was here to experience her first, and probably her only white Christmas.

Treading carefully in her borrowed wellies – Dulcie had loaned her a pair earlier in the week – Eliza walked up the path to the farm. It meant passing through the stable yard, and she spotted Petra and Harry, who were seeing to the horses. Little Amory was with them, dressed in an all-in-one padded suit and bright yellow boots with ducks on them.

'Merry Christmas,' Petra called on seeing her. 'Off up to the farm?'

Eliza chucked the child under his chubby chin. 'Merry Christmas. Yes, I've been invited to lunch.'

'Amos told me you had, otherwise I would have asked you to join us here.'

Eliza's heart swelled. 'That's so kind of you, but I'm sorted. Is this little one pleased with his presents? He's so cute.'

'This 'little one' is a tyrant. He's had us up for hours. Not because he wanted to open his presents, you understand, but because he wanted to go outside and play in the snow. As far as he's concerned, building a snowman is the best present in the world. God help us when the weather turns and it melts. I'm bracing myself for the biggest tantrum ever.'

Eliza giggled. 'I don't blame him. I couldn't wait to play in it, either.' She would never admit it, but she had already built a small snowman of her own in the courtyard outside the cottage, and she'd had immense fun doing it too.

When she arrived at the farm, despite it being only ten o'clock, Eliza discovered that all the lunch preparations had already been done, and no potato peeling was required.

Jay held up his hands and wiggled his fingers. 'See these? Wrinkled from hours spent peeling spuds, so you don't have to,' he teased, before scooping her into a hug. 'Merry Christmas, Eliza.'

The rest of the Fairfaxes plus Walter and Otto followed suit, until she was all hugged out, and when they finally released her, she said, 'I've, um, brought a couple of little gifts,' and she held the bag aloft.

'Aw, you shouldn't have,' Dulcie said, taking it from her. 'Shall I put it under the tree? We've not opened any presents yet, as we thought we'd wait until Nikki, Gio and Sammy got here.'

'Good idea.' Eliza unzipped her coat, beginning to feel rather warm now she was indoors, but Jay stopped her.

'Keep that on, we're going outside,' he said. 'You too, Dulcie. Otto, are you coming?' Jay had a glint in his eye, and Eliza wondered what he was up to.

She soon found out.

The moment she stepped through the door, a snowball hit her on the arm, and Jay had another in his hand, armed and primed. Not to be outdone, Otto bent down to scoop up a handful of snow, and swiftly moulded it into a ball.

Dulcie shot Eliza a look and they nodded to each other. 'Game on!' Dulcie cried and Eliza gave a squeal of joy.

Leaping aside to dodge Jay's next missile, Eliza grabbed a mitten-full of snow and lobbed it at him. It hit him on the shoulder and disintegrated impact, leaving a smudge of white on his jacket. He widened his eyes, a warning that she was about to get as good as she got lurking in their depths, but before he could act on it, another snowball caught him on the chest, thrown by a gleeful Dulcie.

The next few minutes descended into a blur of flying snow and loud squeals and shrieks. At one point, Eliza was aware that Beth and Walter had joined in from the relative safety of the open living room window, but they quickly exhausted the supply of snow on the sill, so resorted to shouting encouragement from the sidelines instead.

The fight ended when Dulcie shoved an icy handful of the white stuff down the back of Otto's neck. With a growl, he picked her up, dumped her into the nearest drift and threw himself down next to her, kissing her until she begged for mercy and surrendered.

'Huh! Dulcie might have thrown in the towel, but I haven't!' Eliza cried. 'I'm still standing.'

Jay's eyes narrowed. 'Not for much longer.'

She realised his intention a fraction before he lunged at her, and she skipped out of reach, before turning with a shriek and racing for the door. He caught her just as she reached it, grabbing her around the waist and pulling her into him.

Eliza squirmed in his grasp, squeaking in mock fear, and then she abruptly froze.

Jay was focusing on a point above her head, and when she followed the direction of his gaze and saw what had caught his attention, she almost melted.

A bunch of mistletoe hung directly above them, and as her eyes dropped to his face, she inhaled sharply.

He was looking at her as though he wanted to eat her all up, and when his head bent and his lips brushed lightly against hers, she would have been more than happy to have let him devour her completely as she sank into his embrace.

Beth's chirpy cry of, 'Sherry, anyone?' broke the mood, and they leapt apart guiltily, Eliza feeling distinctly wobbly. As Dulcie and Otto stepped around them, Dulcie sent Eliza a knowing smirk and Otto lightly punched Jay on the arm and winked.

Eliza and Jay stared at each other. At least this kiss could be blamed on the mistletoe, and although she would dearly love for him to kiss her again, she knew how unwise that would be.

Feeling cold as a trickle of icy snowmelt worked its way down her neck, Eliza shivered.

'Let's get you warmed up,' Jay said, gesturing for her to go ahead of him, but as she took a step into the hall, she shivered again. This time it wasn't because she was cold. It was because of the promise in his eyes. Jay Fairfax wasn't done with her yet – and she couldn't wait.

With her head spinning, her heart racing and her emotions all over the place, Eliza was more than happy to shuck off her wet things and accept a glass of sherry from Beth. She sipped at it gratefully, feeling its rich warmth track down her throat and into her stomach, where it joined the ball of anticipation that was already there.

She avoided looking at Jay, for fear of seeing her own desire reflected back at her, and was relieved when Nikki and her family arrived, Sammy's exuberance giving her something less risky to focus on.

What followed next was an orgy of present-opening, torn wrapping paper and squeals of delight. The two dogs joined in, as they excitedly examined each gift in the hope that it might be for them, so to keep them quiet (Peg was acting like a puppy as she snuffled through the wrapping paper, tearing it to shreds) Walter dug out her and Tara's gifts, and the dogs quickly settled down to gnaw on their fake bones, whilst the humans continued with the unwrapping.

Eliza was touched to discover that the Fairfaxes had clubbed together to buy her a pretty silver necklace and earring from one of the artisan shops in the village, and she was reduced to tears when Walter handed her a small box covered in worn and faded blue velvet.

Inside it was a ring.

'It belonged to my mother, your grandmother,' he said. 'I had no idea why

I've been hanging onto it all these years –
until I met you.'

'Walter, it's too much. I can't accept this.
What about Otto?'

'He's more than welcome to have his
mother's wedding and engagement rings
if he wants them.' Walter glanced at Otto,
then at Dulcie, his meaning clear.

Eliza examined her gift. It was a gold
band with a cushion-cut diamond in the
centre, flanked by two smaller sapphires,
and was absolutely exquisite.

She shook her head. 'I can't take this.'

'You **can**,' Walter insisted. 'I'm sure your
father would have wanted you to have it.'

Ooh, that was a low blow, she thought,
but when she looked at her uncle, she

could see how much it meant to him if she were to accept.

'Thank you,' she said softly and gave him a long hug.

He clung to her, then kissed her cheek. 'I'm so glad you found us.'

'So am I.' She meant it. Being here with Walter, with her new family, in the house her father had once lived in, meant the world to her.

Beth passed Eliza the bag of presents that she had brought with her this morning. 'You'd better give these out, otherwise we'll still be opening presents as Otto is dishing up our dinner.'

Eliza took the bag from her and began handing out the little gifts she'd made. 'I didn't know what to get you,' she said nervously, 'so I hope you like them.'

'I'm sure we will,' Dulcie replied, tearing eagerly at the paper on her present, and when she saw what it was she gave a shriek. 'Look! It's the farm.' She turned the painting around for everyone to see. 'It's perfect. Thank you so much! I really, really love it.'

Eliza breathed a sigh of relief. Thank goodness one of the family liked her gift. She just hoped the rest of them did, too.

One by one, everyone held up the paintings she'd given them: a pastiche of her four children for Beth, a portrait of Otto for Walter, a painting of the boy and his dog for Sammy, a portrait of Sammy holding a chicken (apparently it was his pet chicken) for Nikki and Gio. Otto received a picture of his restaurant and

Eliza could tell that he was thrilled to bits with it, and Maisie was delighted with a watercolour of herself. It showed her face-to-face with the cutest of the pygmy goats, and her rapturous expression was plain to see.

Last but not least, was Jay.

Shyly she handed him the final present. It was obviously a picture of some kind, so she couldn't hide that, but she prayed he liked it and would be able to fit it into his luggage when he returned to Borneo.

His eyes widened when he unwrapped it, and he studied the gift for such a long time that she feared he hated it.

Finally, his gaze sought hers and he smiled, a long slow smile that set her pulse soaring and made her insides melt.

'Thank you,' he mouthed, and placed it on his chest next to his heart.

'Don't keep it to yourself,' his mother said. 'Give us a look.'

Eliza didn't think she imagined his reluctance when he turned it around, although there was nothing controversial about the picture, nothing that was overly personal. It was a portrait of Jay as she had first set eyes on him.

He was standing in the doorway of the abandoned farmhouse on the mountain, and was staring straight out of the picture. It had taken her ages to get his expression right, because for a while she hadn't realised what was lacking. When she finally did, she had painted it in, and now she was fervently praying that no one else realised that she had depicted Jay with hunger in his eyes. From the very first time he'd set those gorgeous blue-green eyes on her, he had wanted her, whether he had known it then or not.

He still wanted her, that much was abundantly clear, and now Eliza wanted him just as fiercely.

The question she had to ask herself was, would she give in? And if she did, could she trust herself not to lose her heart? She knew this could never be anything more than a holiday romance, that they were like ships passing in the night. But should she live for today and enjoy whatever life gave her, or retreat and guard her emotions? She thought of a line from Casablanca, one of her father's favourite films, and realised how compelling it was when Rick had told Isla that they would always have Paris.

If Eliza continued to steel herself against her growing feelings and her undeniable desire for Jay, she would never have her own Paris. She would return to New Zealand and would forever wonder what she had missed.

It was then that she understood that she would regret **not** sharing a few stolen hours with Jay far more than she would regret sharing them. Humphrey Bogart was right...

Jay was Rick, she was Isla, and she wanted her very own Paris here on Muddypuddle Lane.

Jay's emotions were all over the place. The desire on Eliza's face after he had kissed her under the mistletoe had almost sent him into orbit, and he'd had to give himself a stern talking-to. She had been as hungry for more as he, but they were about to open presents and eat lunch with the family, so he'd had to curb his urge to whisk her back to the cottage and make long, languorous love to her.

But when he'd opened the present she'd given him and saw the passion she had captured in his eyes, he had found it hard to keep a lid on things. She had read his hunger even before he'd been aware of it himself, but on looking back to the moment when he had seen her for the first time, he knew she was right. He had wanted her then, and he wanted her now. But did she want him enough to spend the remainder of her time in Muddypuddle Lane with him? After all, she was here to find out more about her father and his family. She wasn't here to be carried off to bed by a man she hardly knew.

There was also something else bothering him.

He liked her. Very much. Too much for this to be a casual roll in the hay. He wanted to get to know her far better than the brief time she had left in the country would allow. He wanted to explore all of her, not just her body – he wanted to explore her mind, too.

And that was what worried him. He had never felt like this about anyone before and he didn't know how to handle it. Should he take whatever she deigned to give and be grateful, whether it be time, friendship, or more…? And if there was more, how would he cope when she left?

He realised he was still standing there with his portrait in his hands and that everyone was staring at him. 'It's fantastic,' he said. 'I love it!' He truly did. Eliza was so incredibly talented.

He saw the relief on her face and smiled.

She smiled back, then caught her bottom lip between her teeth and dropped her gaze. When she glanced back at him from beneath those long lashes of hers, he wondered whether she was flirting with him. When she looked away and then looked back again, he was positive she was.

God! He wished she wouldn't do that. It was sending him wild.

To cover his abrupt surge of lust, he cleared his throat and beckoned her into the dining room. He had contributed to the gift the family had bought, so he didn't want to make an issue of the fact that he'd bought her a present that was purely from him. Hoping not to draw too much attention, he decided to give it to her in private. Or as private as he could get considering Lilac Tree Farm was bursting at the seams with people.

Praying that everyone would stay put in the living room for a couple of minutes, he turned to face Eliza and said huskily, 'I've got something for you,' then wished he hadn't phrased it like that when he saw the amusement in her eyes. 'It's only a little something,' he added, and realised he'd made things worse when she giggled.

He grabbed the festively wrapped package from where he'd stashed it next to the dresser and shoved it at her. 'Here.'

'What is it?'

'Open it and find out.'

Eyes wide, she took it from him and gently eased the paper aside to reveal a wooden tabletop easel with a compartment underneath for paints.

'Look inside,' he urged, and when she opened it she discovered a full array of oils and brushes. 'I asked the woman in the shop to fill it with whatever she thought you might need. I hope it's okay?'

'It's more than okay,' she breathed. 'But this must have cost a fortune.'

'Nah.' He waved a hand in the air. 'Just promise me you'll make good use of it while you're here.'

'I will! Thank you so much!'

She threw her arms around him and he staggered back, but swiftly regained his balance and hugged her to his chest, enfolding her in his arms and breathing in her sweet perfume.

'I want to paint now!' she cried.

Jay chuckled. 'I think Otto will have something to say if you're up to your armpits in paint instead of doing his Christmas dinner justice.' He released her, so she could examine the contents of the box again.

She said, 'I've got so many ideas, I don't know where to start.' Then her face fell. 'Oh…'

'What is it?'

'I'm not going to be able to take the paintings home with me.'

'Whyever not?'

'Oil paints wouldn't have hardened off in time.'

'No worries. Let me know approximately when they'll be ready and I'll ship them for you.'

'But you'll be in Borneo.'

'Um, probably not. Look, keep it to yourself for now, but my contract with the acoustics company ended a couple of weeks ago and it's yet to be renewed. So I'll be in the UK for a while.'

'Will you stay at the farm?'

'Maybe. I don't know. Dulcie and Otto would like the place to themselves, I expect. You've seen what they're like.'

'Will you go stay with your mum?'

'That's another option,' he said, guardedly. He loved his mum to the moon and back, but he couldn't face going to Birmingham.

Otto strode into the room before Jay could say anything further, and as soon Otto spied them he said, 'Come on you two, I could do with a hand in the kitchen. I need to check on the turkey, and while I'm doing that you can put the potatoes on to boil for roasties. Eliza, how good are you at making cranberry sauce?'

'Er...'

'Stuffing?'

'Um...' Eliza pulled a face.

Otto laughed. 'Just kidding. It's already made. But I'm sure Dulcie wouldn't mind you helping her lay the table.'

With an apologetic smile at Eliza, Jay followed Otto into the kitchen. To his surprise the roasties had already been par-boiled and were ready to go in the oven. He sent a questioning look to Otto.

Otto said, 'I wanted to get you on your own for a sec. Sorry, I didn't mean to eavesdrop, but did I hear you say you'd be in the UK for a while?'

'Yeah...'

'What are you going to do about a job?'

Jay shrugged. 'Try to get another contract.'

'What if you don't?'

'Something will turn up.' But the problem was, he wasn't sure whether he wanted to carry on doing what he was doing. He was thirty-four, and anchorless. Aside from a fairly healthy bank balance and a couple of kit bags stuffed with clothes and little wooden carvings, he didn't have much else to his name. Seeing Dulcie with her farm and Otto opening a restaurant, was making him think.

But what else was he equipped to do? Bioacoustics was all he knew.

'I've had the loveliest Christmas Day imaginable,' Eliza announced. She was pleasantly replete, slightly tipsy and full of festive spirit.

It was late – nearly midnight – and Jay was escorting her down the hill back to the cottage. He had one arm around her shoulder and the other was clutching the easel he'd bought her. Despite the falling temperature, she felt warm and cosy (which probably had something to do with the amount of cherry brandy in her system) and she snuggled in closer, loving the feel of his hard body against hers.

'I'm glad,' he said. 'I would have hated for you to be alone on Christmas Day, so far from home.'

Eliza paused, drawing to a halt. 'So would I. If I'm honest, I hadn't really thought this through. I was so focused on getting here and finding Walter, that I hadn't fully appreciated how I might feel being all alone over Christmas. And I was being a bit petty, too.'

They carried on walking.

'In what way?' Jay hugged her into him and his warmth percolated through her jacket and into her body.

'Cathy has always been Mum's favourite, and now that my sister is pregnant, I was feeling even more left out than usual. I was dreading spending Christmas with them. Mum would have fussed over Cathy even more than usual, and what used to be such a happy season when Dad was alive would have been totally miserable. Cathy and Toby – her husband – always spend Christmas with our Mum and New Year with his parents, and Mum would have practically ignored me until they left, then she would have expected me to step into the breach as soon as they'd gone.'

She fished the key out of her pocket and opened the door. A wall of welcome heat rushed out at her. 'I don't even think she knows she's doing it,' Eliza said.

'It still hurts though,' Jay empathised.

'Yes, it does. I know she loves me in her own way, but I'll always be second fiddle to Cathy.' She eased off her coat, and when she held her hand out for Jay's jacket, she hung them side-by-side on the pegs near the door.

'Come here,' she said, pulling him closer. 'I don't want to think about Mum or home right now.' She stared into his eyes and her lips parted.

 His voice was gruff as he said, 'What **do** you want to think about?'

'Nothing. I want you to take me to a place where there is no thought, only feeling. Make love to me, Jay.'

And for a long, long time afterwards, Eliza was blissfully incapable of thinking anything.

CHAPTER EIGHT

Eliza gave Jay a hesitant shake of her head from the passenger seat of his hire car as he asked, 'Are you sure you don't want me to come with you?'

She would dearly like him to accompany her but she didn't want to spook Julia, so she said, 'I'll be fine. Thanks, though.'

'Call me when you're done,' he replied, gathering her to him and kissing her.

'That might be as little as ten minutes, or it could be a couple of hours,' she warned.

'It doesn't matter. Take as long as you need.'

They were parked within sight of the cafe Julia had suggested. Steeling herself, Eliza got out of the car. Wrapping her scarf more tightly around her neck, she hunched deeper into her coat. It was bloody freezing, and she hurried along the pavement and darted into the cafe before her nerves could get the better of her.

Inside was warm, the windows steamy, and she quickly scanned the occupied tables, her disappointment acute when she realised Julia wasn't there. Eliza chose a table near the window, removed her coat and scarf, peeled off her gloves and took a seat. Then she ordered a pot of tea and settled down to wait.

Through the glass she could just make out the bonnet of Jay's car, and a warm glow filled her chest. It was five gloriously wonderful days since they'd first made love on Christmas Day, and she didn't think they'd been apart for more than an hour at a stretch. Jay had spent every night at the cottage, in her arms, and she had revelled in it.

Stubbornly, stupidly, Eliza refused to think of the future, of the undeniable reality that she only had four days left (including this), before she would board the aeroplane and fly out of his life. Four days wasn't long enough. A **lifetime** wouldn't be long enough.

But she had gone into this with her eyes wide open. She had known what she was letting herself in for, that the cost of loving Jay would be gouged out of her broken heart. And still she thought it was a price worth paying, despite the inevitable tears and the inevitable heartache. She would always have Muddypuddle Lane.

The door opened and Eliza sat up straighter as Julia cautiously stepped through it. Breathing a sigh of relief, Eliza lifted her hand in a small wave.

'Can I get you anything?' she asked as Julia took a seat.

'A latte, please.'

Eliza gave the order, then an awkward silence descended. She had no idea how or where to start in asking this woman about her father. And the longer it stretched, the more awkward she felt.

Julia must have felt awkward too, because just as Eliza didn't think she could stand it any longer, Julia blurted, 'I loved him with everything I had. I still do love him, although perhaps not as fiercely as I once did. You don't stop loving someone just because they're dead.'

Eliza gulped. Never had anyone spoken a truer word, and grief clawed at her.

'I loved him so much that I had to let him go,' Julia continued. 'I was married, you see. And pregnant.'

Eliza gasped and clapped a hand to her mouth. Did that mean she had a half-brother or sister out there?

Julia noticed her reaction. 'The baby wasn't his.' She looked up as the waitress placed a cup of steaming coffee in front of her and waited for the woman to retreat before saying, 'You would think that it isn't possible to love two men at the same time, but it is.' She stirred a cube of sugar into her drink, her eyes downcast. 'It's not something I'm proud of, but neither was it something I could control. I fell in love. End of story.'

But it wasn't the end, was it? Eliza wanted to say, but she held her tongue, hoping Julia would fill in the blanks.

Julia finally looked up and sighed. 'I suppose you want to know what happened?'

'Please, if you feel you can talk about it.'

'You deserve to know. Your father – it feels strange to think of Emrys as having children – had already been planning to emigrate to New Zealand before I met him. It was his dream, a new life in a new country. I couldn't take that away from him, but neither could I deprive my husband of his son. If I hadn't been pregnant, I'd have gone with your father in a heartbeat, but I was, so I didn't. Emrys never knew I was carrying Stephen's child. I simply told him that we'd had our fun, but it was over. I never saw or heard from him again. I broke his heart and I'm not sure he ever forgave me.'

'I think he did,' Eliza said slowly. 'Otherwise, why would he have wanted you to know that he'd died, and why did he want you to know that he'd never stopped loving you?'

A tear slid down Julia's face and she brushed it away. 'When you phoned to tell me that he was gone, you said he'd had a good life, that he'd been happy. Is that true?'

'I'd assumed he was. I never really thought about It. He was just my dad, you know? It wasn't until after he died and I found the letter asking me to contact you, that I began to wonder.' Eliza fell silent, thinking. Then she said, 'No, I'm sure he was happy. As you just said, it's possible to love two people at the same time, and I believe he truly loved my mother.'

Julia's reply was soft. 'I'm glad. I still had my husband, you see, and I worried that Emrys wouldn't find anyone to love him as much as I did.'

Eliza said, 'And I'm glad you let him go, because if you hadn't, I wouldn't be here.'

'I want to ask you about his life in New Zealand, about your mother, but I've worked hard to bury it deep, and digging it up again probably isn't a good idea.'

'Probably not,' Eliza agreed.

Julia pushed her untouched coffee away and got to her feet. 'I'm pleased I met you and I'm happy your father found love again, but don't take offence when I say I hope I never see you again.'

'I won't,' Eliza assured her. 'I'm flying back to New Zealand in a few days, so I doubt we will meet again.'

Julia stared at her for a long time, then reached out to pat her on the shoulder. 'Take care, Eliza.'

'You too.' Eliza squeezed Julia's hand, then watched her father's first love walk out of the door.

'Are you okay?' Jay asked. Eliza looked upset. Her generous mouth was downturned, and her eyes swam with unshed tears.

'I'm not sure.'

'Do you want to talk about it?'

Eliza buckled her seatbelt and crossed her arms, hugging herself. 'I've got the feeling my mother knew about Julia. I never told her about the letter Dad left asking me to contact her. I think I guessed even then that it was something I should keep from her. And when I phoned Julia and told her that Dad had died, I knew for sure. Julia was so upset that I honestly believe she loved him deeply. She was married when she and my dad fell in love, but she became pregnant and the baby was her husband's not my dad's. It's quite a sad tale. Dad had already told her it was his dream to emigrate to New Zealand, but she couldn't go with him and I think she guessed he would stay in the UK for her, so she told him she didn't love him. It must have taken a great deal of courage on her part to let him go.'

The tears trickled over, and he reached across and gently wiped them away. 'I should imagine it did.'

The thought occurred to Jay that very soon he wouldn't have to imagine it. He would know firsthand how it felt, because he would be the one to have to let Eliza go. Since that glorious night when he had made love to her for the first time, he hadn't been able to stop thinking of ways they could be together, of how he might persuade her to stay in the UK. But what could he offer her? He didn't have a home of his own and he didn't have a job. Whereas she had both in New Zealand.

It had occurred to him that he could suggest he went with her when she left on Monday (the next four days would be gone far too soon) but how could he, given his circumstances? Besides, he wasn't entirely sure that this wasn't just a flash in the pan for her, a brief fling with a Brit whilst she was on holiday. How would she take it if he suddenly suggested flying out with her? She might be horrified. If he had a job in New Zealand that might be different, but even then, she mightn't want him in her life. He would basically be inviting himself to shack up with her, and that wasn't on. His only option was to make the most of the short time they had left.

Glumly, he started the car and headed for Muddypuddle Lane.

When he arrived at her cottage, he made no move to switch the engine off, aware that Eliza needed time to process what had happened, so when she said, 'I'll see you later,' he let her go without a murmur.

She did lean across the gear stick and give him a kiss on the lips before she got out, so he was somewhat cheered by that.

He said, 'Will you be alright?'

'I'll be fine. There's just something I need to do while it's still fresh in my mind.'

He watched until she had gone inside, then he turned the car around and drove the short distance up the lane to the farm, his heart heavy.

It didn't grow any lighter when he pulled into the yard and saw that the email he'd been waiting for was sitting in his inbox.

He read it twice, then slumped back in his seat and stared into the distance. He'd never been to Belize.

And he wasn't entirely sure he wanted to.

This time last week, he would have leapt at the chance. Now though...

Oh, what the hell? He may as well take the contract. It wasn't as though he had job offers coming out of his ears. And it wasn't as though he and Eliza would be together if he **didn't** take it.

He didn't bother going into the house to change his clothes. The ones he was wearing would do just fine for what he was about to do. Whittling wasn't a particularly grubby pastime, and although the flakes of wood could cling to fabric they would soon brush off.

The goats were pleased to see him and they crowded against the bars of their pen, bleating plaintively.

'I haven't got anything for you,' he told them, stroking the nose of the nearest. She butted him on the hand, a demand for food. 'You've got hay,' he said. 'Eat that.' The creature gave him a disgusted look, as if to say '**You** eat it and see how you like it'.

She was small and white, with little horns and a round belly, and was so damned cute. He could understand how Maisie had fallen in love with her. The others were just as sweet, and he sought out the one who he had been using as his model for the past couple of days.

Unwrapping his tools, he picked up the piece of wood and began to work. The concentration it took was welcome, because it meant he didn't have to think about how he was going to cope when Eliza left.

In some ways, he wished he was leaving first, but his contract didn't start until mid-January, and although he supposed he could fly out early, it wouldn't be early enough. Her flight was on Monday. Today was Thursday. Even if he could get a flight tomorrow, or the next day, he didn't think he would be forgiven if he missed Otto's big night. The Wild Side was due to open on New Year's Eve and Dulcie expected Jay to be there.

After a couple of hours, his sister's voice cut across his thoughts. 'There you are! I wondered where you'd got to. I saw the car in the yard. Is Eliza with you?' She scanned the barn.

'No.' He didn't look up. He was aware he might appear sullen, but he didn't want his face to give away his feelings.

'What's wrong?' Dulcie asked. 'Have you fallen out?'

'No, but it wouldn't make any difference if we had.' He made the mistake of looking at her.

She gave him a shrewd glance. 'Because she's leaving soon?'

He shrugged and carried on shaving slivers of wood off what would eventually become the goat's neck.

His sister continued, 'Why don't you go with her?'

Jay put the knife and the block of wood down, his enthusiasm for the task waning. His reply was simple. 'She hasn't asked me.'

'Ah.' Dulcie paused. She took a step closer and picked up the half-carved piece of wood. 'Goat?' she guessed.

'Uh-huh.'

'You're rather good at wood carving, aren't you?'

'Not really.'

'You **are**,' she insisted. 'The carving of Tara that you gave to Sammy is gorgeous.' She didn't say anything more for a moment, then she asked, 'Would you go with her, if she did?'

'I doubt it.'

'Why not? You love her, that's obvious, and I believe she loves you. So what's stopping you? There's nothing to keep you here. Otto told me you are between contracts at the moment.'

'I had an email this morning. I've been offered another contract.'

'Where?'

'Belize.'

'But what about you and Eliza?'

'There is no me and Eliza. At least, there won't be after Sunday. She lives on the other side of the world, if you remember?'

'She doesn't have to. She could always stay here. So could you.'

'In the UK?'

'In Picklewick. You can stay at the farm for as long as you want. Both of you.'

Jay scowled. 'Thanks, sis, but I can't see that working. For one, I doubt whether Eliza would want to stay. She's got a house, a job and a family in New Zealand. Second, I can't impose. You and Otto need your own space. Besides, I'd want a place of my own if I was going to settle anywhere. And third, if I don't take this contract, I won't have a job.'

It was kind of Dulcie to be so concerned, and even kinder of her to offer for him and Eliza to stay at the farm, but it simply wasn't an option.

Dulcie pursed her lips. 'First, you don't know until you ask. Eliza might jump at the chance to stay here with you. Second, you wouldn't be imposing, but if you insist on having your own place, I've got an idea about that. Third, job-wise you can turn your hand to anything to tide you over, but I've got an idea about that, too.'

'It won't work, Dulcie,' he repeated. He eased his mobile out of his jacket pocket. 'I'm going to email them back and let them know I'm taking the contract.'

His sister opened her mouth, then closed it again. He waited for her to say something, but all she did was kiss him on the forehead, and when she walked out of the barn, Jay didn't think he had ever felt as alone as he did right now.

For a long time he sat on the bale of straw, turning his phone over in his hands, his thoughts a jumbled mess.

God, he was so tempted to take Dulcie up on her offer to stay in Picklewick, but it wouldn't be fair on anyone, him included.

Nope, it was better all round if he took the contract. He'd soon get back into the swing of things, and Eliza would become just a fond memory of a lovely Christmas.

Without dwelling on it any further, Jay sent his acceptance. There, it was done. He would enjoy the rest of his time here and spend as much of it as possible with Eliza.

There was nothing else he could do.

Otto had chosen New Year's Eve for The Wild Side to open its doors for the first time. According to Dulcie, he wasn't charging for the food, just the drinks, and was using the evening purely as an advertisement for the restaurant. Eliza had firsthand experience of how wonderful Otto's cooking was. She guessed if anyone could make a go of it, he could, and she prayed it would be a success.

She hadn't brought anything particularly partyish with her, not expecting to attend any parties, so she'd gone into Thornbury earlier today with Jay to buy something appropriate to wear.

Eliza had discovered a gorgeous little shop down a side street selling all manner of one-off clothes. It was a posh second-hand shop, and she was able to find a gold sparkly dress without a hideous price tag.

Jay had urged her to step out of the fitting room so he could see, but she had refused. She wanted his first sight of her in this dress to be when she was at the restaurant, her hair and make-up done, and she was all glammed up.

So when she shucked off her coat this evening and handed it to one of the waiting staff, the naked admiration on Jay's face gave her a warm glow.

'You look stunning,' he said, kissing her lightly on the lips, careful not to mess her make-up, and his thoughtfulness made her glow some more.

He didn't look too bad himself, dressed as he was in charcoal-coloured chinos and a plain white shirt, open at the neck and with the sleeves rolled up. He looked casual yet smart, confident and sophisticated, and she wanted to eat him all up.

Eliza was pleased to see that everyone had made an effort. Otto was in a tux and Dulcie looked gorgeous in a midnight-blue cocktail dress. Maisie wore something chiffon and floaty, and even

Walter was in a suit and tie, although from the way he plucked at the knot at his neck, Eliza guessed that he didn't dress up very often, and she giggled, making a bet with herself that he would take the tie off within the hour.

There were several people Eliza recognised, such as Lena, Amos's partner, and Charity who helped out at the stables. She was here with her boyfriend Timothy, a local vet, and Eliza did a double take, fearing that the bubbly she was drinking was spiked when she saw two of her, before realising that Charity had a twin sister.

There were also many people she didn't recognise, and to Eliza it seemed as though the whole village was here to offer their support.

Jay slipped an arm around her waist. 'It's a good turn-out,' he said. 'And I don't think it's just because of the free food. Otto spent today and yesterday preparing a buffet for the opening, so he doesn't have to spend the whole evening in the kitchen.'

Eliza didn't think so either. There was a real sense of community spirit and support, and she was amazed at the way everyone rallied around, when she couldn't even get her mother or her sister to rally around her.

Jay said, 'I can't believe how well Dulcie has settled in. It's as though she's been a part of Picklewick all her life. Otto, too; even though he grew up on the farm on Muddypuddle Lane, he had lived away for many years. No wonder Nikki decided to make the village her home.'

Eliza spotted Jay's eldest sister laughing up at Gio, and she smiled. 'I think a certain policeman might also have played a part in that decision.'

Dulcie had told her about Sammy being bullied in his school in Birmingham, and how he had run away to the farm. Dulcie had also told Eliza about how Nikki had fallen in love with Gio last summer, but Dulcie hadn't imagined anything would come of it considering Nikki lived in the city and Gio lived in Picklewick. But then Gio had asked Nikki and her son to move in with him and the rest, they say, is history.

Eliza couldn't fail to compare Nikki's situation to her own – minus the child, of course. Her and Jay's relationship was also a holiday romance, but the biggest difference was, she lived on the other side of the world. It was going to break her heart when she had to say goodbye to him.

But what if he asked her to stay in Picklewick? Would she? **Could** she?

Eliza thought of her little bach near the beach, of the sunlight flooding into her studio, of the beauty of the bay and the peace she enjoyed, and her slowly growing reputation as an artist. Could she give up everything she had fought so hard for, for love?

And suddenly she knew, without any doubt, that she could, that if Jay asked her to stay, she would.

Then she glanced down at her glass and thought the alcohol must have gone to her head, because what she was thinking was absolute nonsense. Jay wouldn't be staying here either; he was off to Belize at the end of next week, which was roughly eleven thousand kilometres from New Zealand. She knew because she'd looked it up.

She also knew something else – that she was in love with him. She had lost her heart to Jay as she suspected she might. And when midnight came and everyone cried 'Happy New Year!' Eliza wondered just how happy this new year could possibly be without the man she had fallen in love with.

CHAPTER NINE

'A picnic? Won't it be chilly?' Eliza looked doubtful.

'Humour me?' Jay urged. This was their final day together and he wanted to pay homage to the first time he met her. He wanted to take her back to the abandoned farmhouse high on the mountain above, because even though he hadn't realised it at the time, that was where he had fallen in love with her.

Eliza said, 'I suppose we can't stay in bed **all** day. But isn't Dulcie expecting us for lunch?'

On hearing those words, Jay nearly changed his mind. All day in bed sounded wonderful, and he briefly debated suggesting that they hide under the duvet and refuse to answer the door. Dulcie was insisting that everyone enjoyed a final meal together, a New Year's Day lunch to rival the Christmas Day feast, and Jay and Eliza were expected to attend.

But Jay wanted Eliza all to himself for as long as possible, and the only way to ensure that had been to tell Dulcie that he and Eliza were going out for the day. Dulcie had reluctantly pushed lunch back to dinnertime, and had told him that if he didn't show up, he would have their mother to answer to. Her final piece of guilt-tripping had been to tell him that Eliza needed to say a proper goodbye to Walter and the rest of her new-found family, because not only was Eliza going home tomorrow, but so were Beth and Maisie.

'Lunch is at 6 o'clock now, so we've got plenty of time to go for a walk,' he told her.

'I need to pack,' she said, glancing around the bedroom.

Jay swallowed. 'How about you make a start on that, and I'll pop back to the farm to change, and I can rustle up a picnic while I'm there.'

He had already asked Otto to pack up some of the leftover buffet food from last night and bring it home with him, so it shouldn't take more than a few minutes. He hated being away from her for even that short length of time.

How he was going to cope when he would be away from her permanently, was something he didn't want to think about.

Jay hurried up the track to the farm and barrelled in through the door, almost sending Dulcie flying in his haste to get to the kitchen.

'Whoops, sorry.' His hand shot out to steady her.

She said, 'I was hoping to catch you. Are you in a hurry? I'd like to run something by you.'

'A bit. I'm taking Eliza for a picnic, remember? Do you have any hot water bottles?'

'Um, I think so. Try the pantry. Top shelf.'

Jay trotted into the kitchen, Dulcie following.

He said, 'Can you put the kettle on and fill them up for me, while I sort the food out? Oh, and I'll need to borrow a couple of blankets, if I can.'

Dulcie shook her head but flipped the switch on the kettle and rummaged around in the pantry, yelling, 'Ta-dah!' when she emerged with a pair of hot water bottles.

'What do you want to run by me?' Jay asked, his head in the fridge as he sorted through various Tupperware boxes of buffet food. There hadn't been much left over, but there was enough for him and Eliza to have a nice picnic.

Dulcie put a hand on his arm, and he looked over his shoulder. Her expression was serious. 'You don't have to go to Belize, you know. You don't **have** to take that contract if you don't want to.'

Jay stifled a sigh. 'We've been through this,' he began, but his sister said, 'Hear me out,' so he subsided and turned to face her.

She continued, 'I've been thinking... What if you had a place of your own in Picklewick? Would you stay?'

'It's a moot point. I **don't** have a place of my own, and even if I did, I don't have a job remember?'

'You can make things and sell them,' Dulcie said.

'Like what?'

'Your carvings. Don't get annoyed, but I've made some enquiries at the shop in the village that sells lots of little handmade crafty stuff, and they said they'd be happy to stock some of yours on a commission basis.'

Jay was taken aback. 'I can't see that working. I'd have to shift an awful lot of carvings to afford to pay the rent on even an outhouse in Picklewick, and before you suggest it again, I'm not going to move in with you and Otto.'

'I'm going to need help on the farm,' she persisted, 'and I'd prefer to employ you than a stranger. Otto wants to turn one of the outbuildings into a pasteurisation shed, and that's not going to be cheap. He suggested that you could help in exchange for board and lodge.'

'I'd still be living with you.'

'Would that be so bad? Anyway, it mightn't be for long.' Dulcie took a breath and stared him in the eye. 'You know that old abandoned farmhouse on the top of the mountain?'

Jay blinked at the sudden change of topic. 'That's where me and Eliza are going for our picnic. Has the kettle boiled yet?'

Dulcie didn't so much as glance at it. She continued to stare at him, her expression serious. 'It's yours if you want it.'

'Hurry up, Dulcie. I want to get up there before it gets dark,' he said, taking a couple of plastic tubs out of the fridge and checking the contents. Then he froze. 'What did you say?'

'It's yours, if you want it,' she repeated. 'It'll be a lot of work and I don't even know if it's doable, or if you need planning permission, and there's no electricity so you'll have to be off-grid, but there is water and I'm sure you can—'

'Stop there.' Jay held up his hand. 'What do you mean **it's mine if I want it?** How can it be mine?'

'I own it. It's part of the farm, but if you want it, you can have it.'

Jay slumped against the worktop in shock. '**Mine?** As in, you're **giving** it to me?'

She pulled a face. 'I'm never going to use it. It needs too much work.'

'I should say so – it's practically a ruin. You'd be better off knocking it down and starting again.'

'That's for you to decide.'

He gazed at her incredulously. 'You're serious.'

'Yes, I am.'

'But...'

'Think about it. The offer is there.' She bit her lip. 'I'm not sure what Eliza would make of it though. It's a bit... rustic.'

'It's a bit derelict.' Jay puffed out his cheeks. 'It's a lovely offer, sis, and I appreciate it, but there's no point in me staying in the UK.'

'Because Eliza won't be here?'

'You've got it in one.'

Eliza was amazed to see how much snow remained on the hillside. It hadn't quite disappeared from the lower slopes yet, but it was all slushy and the roads were totally clear, yet up here it was ankle-deep on the track and had drifted to knee-deep in places. It had also started to snow again, large flakes falling from a cloud-filled sky, and part of her was praying that the flakes would turn into a blizzard and she would be snowed in and unable to get to the airport tomorrow.

But then, would it be worse if she had to psych herself up to leave all over again in a few days?

Tears pricked behind her eyes at the thought of leaving, and she hurriedly blinked them away, hoping Jay didn't spot them. If he did, she'd blame her watery eyes on the cold.

Surprisingly, she didn't feel particularly cold right now. The hike up the hill was keeping the blood pumping, and if it hadn't been snowing she might have considered taking a layer off.

It was a different matter when they reached the abandoned building though, because as soon as she stopped moving, she could feel the chill settling into her bones.

'First things first, let me get a fire started,' Jay said, and her mouth dropped open when he retrieved kindling, newspaper and several briquettes from the rucksack he was carrying.

She watched, bemused, as he pulled a blanket out of the large rucksack he was carrying, along with a couple of hot water bottles. He gave one to her, then spread the blanket on the stones for her to sit on.

As soon as she was settled and had assured him that she was warm enough, he set about making the fire, and before long flames were crackling in the little makeshift hearth he had created, and was kicking out a surprising amount of heat.

Jay joined her on the blanket. 'Are you hungry?'

She wasn't, but she said she was because he had gone to so much effort and she didn't want to disappoint him by not eating.

He passed her a tub of goodies, and she opened them and popped a tiny tartlet in her mouth. The flavours were incredible and she quickly ate it, then another, and when he unscrewed the cap on a thermos flask and poured steamy tomato soup into a mug, she took it eagerly.

They ate in silence, the falling snow blanketing any noise from the world outside their little shelter, and Eliza wished that this moment would never end. She wasn't prepared to return to reality. She wasn't prepared to let Jay go.

But let him go she must... and this time tomorrow she would be far away from the farm on Muddypuddle Lane and getting further away with every step of her journey.

Ever since Dulcie had informed him that the ramshackle, abandoned old farmhouse was his if he wanted it, Jay hadn't been able to think about anything else. Sitting in the middle of it with Eliza by his side, he could picture them sitting in the same spot this time next year. The walls surrounding them would be whole once again, and there would be glass in the windows and a roof over their heads. They wouldn't need much, just the basics – as long as they had each other, that would be enough.

Once or twice he almost plucked up the courage to ask her to stay, but when she shivered and brushed a snowflake from her forehead, he realised it was a pipe dream. It would take months, if not years, to make this place habitable again, and that was assuming he would be granted planning permission. Although he had savings, he estimated that the money in his bank account would quickly be eaten up, even if he managed to do some of the renovation himself. Materials were expensive, and there would be some tasks (**many** tasks) that would be beyond his skill set. A bit of whittling didn't a carpenter make. Or a roofer. Or an electrician.

Eliza was snuggling up next to him and staring into the flames, but instead of concentrating on her, Jay's mind was on the issue of access to the property. The overgrown dirt track would quickly become a mud bath as soon as anything heavier than a human came into contact with it, and he had visions of having to tarmac it before work on the building could even start.

No, Dulcie, he thought, thinking fondly of his kind, well-meaning sister, it would take a better man than him to tackle such a daunting project.

But even as he decided that it was a daft idea, he couldn't help toying with it, turning it over and over in his mind, examining it from every angle and wondering whether it could work.

'Eliza, I—'

A shrill jangle made him jump, and for a moment he couldn't work out where the noise was coming from until he saw Eliza slip her glove off and ferret around in her pocket. He had almost forgotten she had a mobile phone, so rarely did she use it.

She examined the screen. 'I've had a couple of missed calls from my mother,' she said worriedly. 'She's left me a voicemail. Oh, god, I hope it's not bad news.' Hurriedly, she stabbed at the phone then held it to her ear.

Jay looked on in concern, seeing her expression change from alarm to bewilderment, then to delighted.

When she let out a squeal, he jumped. 'What is it?'

'I've just had the most brill news!' she cried. 'I can't believe it.' She was beaming, her eyes bright with joy. 'Apparently, a minor celebrity spotted some of my paintings in Arty Smarty, a small out-of-the-way gallery in Aukland, and she bought a couple. She posted about how much she loved them on social media, and the art gallery has had loads of interest. So much interest that they've sold every single one of my paintings and want to know how soon I can supply them with more!' She squealed again. 'Ooh, I can't believe it! Mum said they've been trying to get hold of me and when they couldn't, they contacted her because they knew I was her daughter.' She studied her phone, scrolling rapidly. 'Blimey, I did have a couple of emails last week, but they've gone into my spam folder.' Eliza blew out her cheeks. 'Thank god they contacted my mum... Ooh, I'm so happy!' She hugged herself with excitement, screwing her eyes tightly shut.

He was thrilled for her, and he knew how much it meant to her that her mother approved of her art. But how could he ask Eliza to stay with him in Muddypuddle Lane now?

With the decision taken out of his hands, Jay's heart ached anew as the realisation that they only had a few short hours left stabbed him in the chest.

How was he going to carry on without her?

Eliza thought she must be all sobbed out, but she was wrong. With every hug and every kind word or kiss on the cheek, she burst into tears all over again.

'I'm going to miss you all so much,' she wept, as Beth swept her into an embrace and hugged her fiercely, until Walter wrestled her free for another hug.

'You especially,' she told him.

'Give my regards to your mother and sister,' he said, 'and come back as soon as you can. I mean it – there'll always be a home for you on Muddypuddle Lane.'

'I can't believe I'm leaving,' she wailed. 'I feel like I've known you forever.'

'In a way, you have,' Walter replied, patting her back as he held her. 'Emrys and I weren't all that different.'

Eliza cried even harder, and didn't stop until she had bundled herself into her coat and stumbled outside for her final walk to the little cottage that had been her home for the last couple of weeks.

As she and Jay made their way down the hill, Eliza's tears dried up, replaced by a sadness so deep she feared it might be bottomless.

In six hours she would be gone, and she didn't know if she would ever be back, despite her promise to Walter, because she didn't think she could face Muddypuddle Lane if Jay wasn't there. He was flying to South America on Friday, and she didn't know if she would ever see him again.

They made beautiful bittersweet love for hours that night. He was tender and sad, gazing into her eyes with such intensity she felt as though he was sinking into her very soul. He couldn't get enough of her, nor she him.

Eventually though, he fell asleep, his arms wrapped around her, whilst she lay wide awake, imprinting those final moments on her memory.

When the time came, she eased herself out of his embrace and crept noiselessly from the bedroom, to dress hurriedly in the dark silence.

He hadn't realised that her case and carry-on were in the living room; he hadn't noticed that her travelling clothes had been placed neatly on the sofa. Or if he had, the significance had passed him by. Because if he had guessed that she was planning on slipping away in the middle of the night, Eliza doubted whether he would have let her go without saying goodbye.

He'd wanted to drive her to the airport himself. But Eliza couldn't cope with a tearful farewell at check-in.

This way was better for both of them. He would wake to find her gone, the only physical reminder that she had ever been there would be the self-portrait she left for him and the note.

She hoped he would forgive her.

Quietly, she let herself out of the cottage, her face damp with tears, and made her way to the lane where the taxi she had ordered would be waiting to take her away from Muddypuddle Lane, her new family, and the man who had stolen her heart.

Jay's arms were empty. There was no soft warm body pressed against him, no head on his chest, and he abruptly surfaced from a fitful slumber where he had been dreaming of wandering through the jungle, calling Eliza's name.

It took him a second or two to realise that the cottage was unnaturally silent, and a few seconds longer to scramble out of bed and stumble downstairs.

But there was no sign of the woman he loved.

She was gone. All that was left of her was a painting and a note.

Jay read it in disbelief, the pain of losing her slamming into him. Even though he understood her reason for sneaking away in the night, he berated her for denying him a few more precious hours with her.

If he hurried, he could—

He sighed, his heart a stone of agony in his chest, and slowly returned to the bedroom to dress. It was over.

It had run its course, as it had always been destined to.

He had to let it go.

Jay wondered where she was now and what time she had left. Was she thinking about him at this very moment? Or was her mind focused on her journey and what awaited her at the other end.

He hoped she would be happy. He hoped she would think of him occasionally.

He hoped that given time, he would recover from loving her.

Another departure faced him when he walked into the farmhouse. His mother and Maisie were also leaving today. His mother appeared resigned. His sister, not so much.

'Can't we stay another week?' Maisie was asking as he stumbled into the kitchen.

'Why?' His mother was sitting at the table eating breakfast. Maisie was leaning against the fridge, nursing a mug of coffee.

'Because it's fun here,' his sister said.

'It was fun because it was Christmas. Christmas is over. It's back to normal now,' Beth pointed out.

'I don't like normal,' Maisie pouted. 'Not my version of it.'

'Some days I'm not too keen on my version, either,' Beth retorted tersely. She turned to Jay. 'What time are you leaving to take Eliza to the airport?'

His reply was clipped. 'I'm not. She's already left.'

'I could stay here?' Maisie's voice was hopeful.

'And do what?'

Jay made himself a coffee that he didn't want, but thought he had better try to drink. If nothing else, the routine was familiar and it might prevent him from breaking down – for a couple of minutes, at least.

Maisie rolled her eyes. 'I dunno. I'll find something. I always do.'

'And you lose it again, just as fast.' Their mother's reply was sharp.

Maisie glanced at Jay for support.

Jay had none to give. Mum was right. Maisie was good at getting a job. Not so good at keeping it.

In a huff, his sister stalked out of the kitchen, and a second later he heard her heavy tread as she stomped upstairs.

His mum said, 'I despair of that girl ever growing up. She's twenty-five, going on fifteen.' She pushed her plate away, the toast half-eaten, and when she looked up at him, Jay realised she was close to tears.

'She'll find her place in the world,' he said. 'It's taking her a bit longer than the rest of us, that's all.'

'Remind me, where's **your** place this time?' Beth sniffed and withdrew a tissue from her pocket.

'Belize. South America.'

'So far away…' A tear escaped, trickling down her cheek.

His heart broke afresh to see it. 'Don't cry, Mum. I'll try to come home in the summer.'

'I'm not crying about that. I'm upset because you let love slip through your fingers.'

Jay stiffened. 'I don't know what you're talking about.'

'I think you do. I know you too well, Jay Fairfax.'

He conceded defeat. There was little point in trying to pull the wool over his mother's eyes. He'd never been any good at that and she'd always seen straight through him. 'It wouldn't work,' he said.

'Why not?'

'She's got her life in New Zealand, I've got mine in—'

'Belize? Borneo? Sumatra?' she interrupted. 'You can make your life wherever you want.'

'I can't. I go where they send me, where the work is.'

'Work isn't everything, my boy.'

'That's not what you say to Maisie.'

'**She's** not about to make the biggest mistake of her life.' His mother's tears had dried, but her expression remained sad.

'I know what I'm doing,' he replied, his untouched coffee going cold.

'I doubt that.'

Exasperated, he growled, 'What do you suggest, Mum? I can't ask her to go to Belize with me. For one thing, I'll be in the middle of the jungle so it's not the easiest environment to live in, and for another, she's got a home and a family in New Zealand.'

'If she won't – or can't – go with you, it's up to you to go with her.'

Jay barked out a laugh. 'To **New Zealand?** What if she doesn't want me to? She left in the middle of the night – I was supposed to be driving her to the airport, remember?'

Beth tutted. 'Oh, for goodness sake, I expect she did that because she didn't want you to see how upset she was. How long will it take to get to Heathrow?'

Jay replied automatically, 'Three or four hours, depending on the traffic.'

'Then what are you waiting for?'

He blinked. 'You think I should go after her?'

'Don't **you?**'

'Well, yes, but—'

'Stop making excuses. If you want her, go get her. If you can't live without her, you need to tell her so. And if you have to give up your new life in some godforsaken jungle so you can be live hers, then that's what you'll have to do.'

'I can't just—'

'You **can!**' His mother got to her feet, took the mug out of his hand and propelled him towards the door. 'If you don't, you'll always think **what if…** and you don't want to be doing that for the rest of your life. Get a move on,' she urged. 'You've got to get to her before she goes through security, because if she does that she won't be spat back out until she gets to the other end.'

She was right, he realised. He **would** regret it. He had to try.

Impulsively, he swept his mother into a hug.

'Text me,' she ordered when he released her.

'I will,' he promised.

His last sight of her as he raced out of the room was her satisfied face as she called after him, 'You better had,' followed by, 'My bloody kids will be the death of me one of these days.'

Jay was packed and on the road in fifteen minutes.

The world outside the window of the train looked as dreary as Eliza felt. She was exhausted, heartbroken and so utterly sad that she felt like howling. Instead, she settled for a plastic cup of dishwater coffee, and tried not to wonder whether Jay was awake yet.

The thought of him slumbering on in the cottage, oblivious to her having already left, made her tummy turn over. What would he think? Would he hate her for running out on him? Would he be relieved not to have to face such an emotional farewell at the airport?

She would probably never know.

Compulsively, she checked her mobile for the umpteenth time since she'd left Muddypuddle Lane, half-hoping to see a message from him.

Jay hadn't messaged her, but her mother had. Call me as soon as you get this. Urgent.

Eliza felt a stab of guilt. She should have replied to her mother yesterday, but she had been a little preoccupied. She had managed to email the gallery though, although she wouldn't get a reply yet because today and tomorrow were national holidays back home.

As soon as her mother answered, Eliza began, 'Hi, Mum, I got your message and I emailed the gallery. Thanks for letting me know the good news. They did try to—'

'That's not why I wanted to speak to you,' her mother broke in. 'I've just had your uncle on the phone.'

It took Eliza a second to realise who she meant. '**Walter?**'

'The very same. Look, I can't pretend to understand what you've been up to, but he's worried about you. He thinks you're making a big mistake. He mentioned a man called Jay? What's going on, Eliza?'

Wait... **Walter** had phoned her **mother**? About her and Jay? **What on earth?!**

'Who is Jay?' her mother demanded. 'And what's this mistake you are supposed to be making?'

'It's a long story. I'm on the train at the moment. I'll tell you about him when I get home.'

'You'll tell me about him **now**.' Her mother's tone brooked no argument.

Eliza bowed to the inevitable and began to explain. 'Walter doesn't own the farm now, a woman called Dulcie does. Jay is her brother.'

'How old is he? What does he do?'

'He's thirty-four and he works in bioacoustics.'

'Do you love him? Walter seems to think you do.'

Eliza sucked in a breath. 'Yes.'

'This is like Barry Skomer all over again.'

'Hardly,' Eliza huffed. 'I'm not about to move to Galway, buy a boat and take up crab fishing for a living.'

There was a pregnant pause, and then her mother spoke. 'The beauty of doing what you do, is that you can do it anywhere.'

'Do you mean paint?'

'You don't need to take up fishing, or find a job in a bar, or pick fruit for a living. You can paint your pictures anywhere. You can sell them anywhere.'

That wasn't strictly true, but Eliza knew what her mother was getting at. A thought suddenly occurred to her. 'Mum, how did the gallery know I'm your daughter?'

'I told them.'

'But... you never visit galleries.' Eliza didn't add, **not even the ones where your daughter's work is displayed.**

'I visited this one.'

'Why?'

'Because they were selling your paintings and I wanted to see them.'

Eliza was flabbergasted. 'You don't **like** my paintings,' she protested.

'I do. It was painting as a career I wasn't keen on. I thought it was too precarious;

but I've been proved wrong. You're good. Very good.'

Eliza swallowed the lump that had formed in her throat. 'I thought you hated it because—' she began without thinking, then stopped abruptly, not wanting to have that discussion right now.

Her mother guessed what she had been about to say. 'Because it reminded me of where your father grew up? Of everything that happened before he came to New Zealand?'

'Well, yes,' Eliza admitted, her heart in her mouth.

'I never hated that you painted. I wasn't keen on it purely because it's not a secure career. And I'll also admit to feeling a bit left out. It was something you and your dad had in common.'

'Dad never painted.'

'I know, but your grandmother did. You reminded him of her.' Her mum paused again. 'Did you find what you were looking for in Picklewick?'

Eliza smiled sadly. She had, and a whole lot more besides. 'I feel closer to Dad,' she said. 'Walter reminds me of him so much. Sometimes, when the light is right, or he holds himself in a certain way, it's like Dad is still with me.'

'Your father will always be with you, Eliza. Never forget that.' She sighed deeply. 'I miss him every day.'

'Me too,' Eliza said.

Her mum chuckled softly. 'He was so proud of you. As am I.'

Eliza was welling up. She had waited a very long time to hear her mum tell her that she was proud of her, and she bit her lip to stop herself from bursting into tears. She had already done so much crying over this past day or so.

'Anyway,' her mother said briskly, clearly back to business. 'Tell me more about Jay.'

'There's not much to tell. We met. I fell in love. He's off to Central America on Friday, I'm on my way home. End of story.'

'Do you *want* it to be the end of your story?'

'No, but—'

'Does he know that?'

'No, but–'

'Then you need to tell him,' her mother urged. 'As a general rule, men have to have things spelt out to them. Sometimes daughters do, too. Where is he now?'

'Um, Picklewick?'

You need to go back.'

'I'll miss my flight.'

'You can get another. What you can't always get is another chance of happiness. Go buy your boat, Eliza...'

Eliza got off the train at the next stop.

'Dulcie, what do you want? I'm driving.' Jay kept his eyes on the road as he spoke.

'I know. You've got to come back to Picklewick.'

'Sorry. Can't. I'm on my way to the airport.'

'Yes, I know, Mum told me. But you have to turn around. Eliza isn't going to Heathrow.'

Jay faltered, his speed dropping. 'Where **is** she going?'

She's coming back to Picklewick.'

'Excuse me?'

'You heard. She's not catching her plane today. She's on her way back to the farm.'

'You're joking!' His brain had frozen and he was struggling to get to grips with what his sister was telling him.

'I most definitely am not!'

'How do you know?' He was aware he sounded suspicious, but this was so surprising that he suspected something must be up.

'Walter spoke to Eliza's mother and got her to phone Eliza. I don't know what she said, but whatever it was, Eliza decided she had to come back. Isn't that wonderful?'

Jay hoped it might be, but he wasn't entirely convinced. It all depended on **why** Eliza was coming back.

Then he decided he didn't care about the reason. He was going to see her again – that's what mattered.

Dulcie was saying, 'Eliza's mother called Walter back to tell him that Eliza was on her way, and he told me, and now I'm telling you.'

Jay didn't need to hear it again.

With a heart filled with hope, he came off the motorway at the next junction and headed back to the place he was beginning to think of as home.

But he didn't drive straight to Picklewick – there was someplace else he needed to be first.

Eliza dragged her suitcase off the train, hoisted her carry-on onto her shoulder and walked towards the exit. It wasn't a particularly large station and very few people had got off at this stop, so the platform was almost deserted.

Apart from one solitary figure at the far end, near the steps.

A man was standing there, watching her.

She swallowed hard and came to a halt, her heart thumping, her knees suddenly feeling too wobbly to hold her up.

Eliza hadn't expected to see Jay here. She had expected to find him at the farm, where she would try to tell him how much she loved him, and that their love deserved a chance. She didn't care where she went, or what she did, as long as they could be together.

Hesitantly, she began walking towards him.

He took several steps towards her.

As he grew closer, she could see the love and fear in his eyes, and she guessed those emotions were reflected in her own.

'You came back,' he said, stopping a few feet away.

'I did. You came to meet me...'

'I did.' The corners of his mouth lifted in a tiny smile.

'How did you know I'd be here?' she asked, baffled.

'Walter, your mum, Dulcie.'

'Ah. '

'Eliza, I—' he began, just as she said, 'Jay, I—'

They both stopped talking. He pulled a face, and she bit her lip.

'I love you,' he blurted, at the same time she stammered those very words to him.

Then suddenly she was in his arms, his lips had found hers, and they were kissing frantically, furiously, neither of them wanting to let go.

Finally, another train pulled into the opposite platform, and Eliza became aware that they had an audience, and she reluctantly dragged her mouth away from his.

'What happens now?' she asked, uncertainty washing over her. It was all well and good for them to declare their love, but what were they going to **do?**

'No idea,' he replied cheerfully. 'All I know is that I don't want to spend my life without you. We'll work the rest out as we go along.'

Eliza was content with that. After all, if she hadn't returned to Picklewick, she knew she would have regretted it for the rest of her life. And who would want to live a life of regret? Who would want to settle for Paris when she had the whole world in her hands?

This Christmas had truly been a Christmas to remember, and no matter where she and Jay went, or where they lived, the farm on Muddypuddle Lane would always hold a special place in Eliza's heart.

Blimey it's warm, Eliza thought, swiping a strand of hair away from her face with her forearm. April was normally when the temperature started to drop, but the North Island was having an Indian summer. According to Jay's mother when she had spoken to her on the phone yesterday, she said they were having some good weather in the UK, too.

Eliza finished preparing the patties and took the tray out to Jay, who was on the veranda tending to the barbeque. Her mum was sitting in a deck lounger, sipping the cocktail he had made her. She looked very much at home, and it warmed Eliza's heart to see it.

Someone else also warmed her heart, and that was Jay. Actually, he made it sing with joy, and she was astounded to think she could be this happy. It was positively obscene how in love she was. And if he was to be believed (and she had no reason to doubt him), Jay was just as besotted with her.

It had taken much discussion, but eventually they had settled in New Zealand. As much as Eliza had adored her stay in Picklewick, this was her home, and she simply couldn't imagine living in Belize – even if it wouldn't be forever.

Jay hadn't batted an eyelid when she'd said she wanted to return to her little bach near the beach. He had simply bought a plane ticket and packed up his things. Amongst them were his wood carving tools, and the first thing he'd done when he saw her gorgeous little studio was to build a workshop next to it, where she could see him from her easel as she painted, whittling away, his head bowed as he concentrated. She was delighted that there had already been some interest in his work...

Jay beamed at her as he turned the patties on the barbie, and she grinned back. He looked so happy and relaxed, and handsome... **let's not forget handsome,** she thought.

'He's not a bad-looking bloke, your Jay,' her mother said, noticing the direction of Eliza's gaze. 'You've done alright for yourself. I was telling Cathy that very thing the other day, and she agreed. She said he's a keeper, and you don't want to let him go.'

Neither her sister nor her mother needed to worry on that score, because Eliza had no intention of letting him go. It had taken a flight to the other side of the world for her to find her soulmate...

Eliza put a hand on her stomach and smiled secretly to herself. They would definitely return to Picklewick though, because she couldn't wait to introduce the baby to his or her family on Muddypuddle Lane.

There are loads more large print books in the Muddypuddle Lane series. Available at all good book stores, or ask your local library.

About Etti

Etti Summers is the author of wonderfully romantic fiction with happy ever afters guaranteed.

She is also a wife, a mum, a pink gin enthusiast, a veggie grower and a keen reader.